STORYTIME
For the Very Young

STORYTIME
For the Very Young

Hilary Turner

Illustrated by
Charlotte Matthews

The Book Guild Ltd.
Sussex, England

For Ashley and George

This book is a work of fiction. The characters and situations in this story are imaginary. No resemblance is intended between these characters and any real persons, either living or dead.

This book is sold subject to the condition that it shall not, by way of trade or otherwise, be lent, re-sold, hired out, photocopied or held in any retrieval system, or otherwise circulated without the publisher's prior consent in any form of binding or cover other than that in which this is published and without a similar condition including this condition being imposed on the subsequent purchaser.

The Book Guild Ltd.
25 High Street,
Lewes, Sussex.

First published 1991
© Hilary Turner 1991
Set in Souvenir Light
Typesetting by Ashford Setting & Design,
Ashford, Middlesex.
Printed in Great Britain by
Antony Rowe Ltd.,
Chippenham, Wiltshire.

British Library Cataloguing in Publication Data
Turner, Hilary
 Storytime
 I. Title II. Matthews, Charlotte
 823.914 [J]

ISBN 0 86332 531 9

CONTENTS

The Lazy Squirrel	7
Mr Smith's Black Hat	11
A Home in the Oak Tree	14
The Little Red Bicycle	17
The Yellow Umbrella	21
The Little Blue Tractor	25
Mr Blue Tit Goes House Hunting	29
The Lost Baby Blackbird	33
The Noisy Donkey	36
Colin the Lonely Crane	39
The Five Ducklings	42
New Homes for Baby Rabbits	48
Poppet the Puppy	52
The Ripe Red Apple	57
The Enormous Puddle	61
A Mouse in the House	65
A Day at the Seaside	71
Billy the Barge	75
Sidney the Snail	80
The Happy Snowman	84

The Lazy Squirrel

ALL THROUGH THE hot summer six little squirrels played in the wood. They raced each other to the tops of the tallest trees and played hide and seek among the green leaves. At night they slept in their snug dreys high in the tree tops. All through the hot summer six little squirrels had so much fun!

At the end of the summer cool winds started to blow through the branches of the trees. The dusty green leaves started to turn yellow, red and orange. Shiny acorns and sweet hazelnuts ripened among the leaves. Soon the leaves started to flutter down, and the acorns and hazelnuts dropped one by one onto the piles of leaves on the ground.

One cool morning six little squirrels stopped playing and one of them said: 'The summer is over. We must collect plenty of nuts and acorns and store them away in secret places. Then, during the cold winter when the ground is hard and nothing grows, we will have plenty to eat.'

Five little squirrels scampered away. They ran this way and that, up and down trees and through piles of dead leaves, picking up acorns and nuts. They hid them in secret places among the high branches. One little squirrel felt rather lazy. He said:

'That isn't fun
I'm going to play
I'll gather my acorns
another day.'

He ran through the wood and into a field. He met a rabbit digging a burrow. The rabbit said:
'Hello little squirrel. Shouldn't you be busy collecting nuts for the winter?'
The squirrel said:

'That isn't fun
I'm going to play
I'll gather my acorns
another day.'

So the squirrel and the rabbit played all day. They chased each other round and round the burrows and through the long grass.
At last the squirrel was tired and he ran home. Five little squirrels were already asleep. They had had a busy day collecting acorns and nuts and they were very tired. The lazy squirrel crept into his drey and fell asleep.
The next day five little squirrels said:

'Come with us.
There is so much to do
gathering nuts
for the whole winter through.'

But the lazy squirrel said:

'That isn't fun
I'm going to play
I'll gather my acorns
another day.'

So he ran away through the wood. There was a stream at the edge of the wood. The squirrel stopped there and met a frog

sitting on the muddy bank. The frog croaked:
'Hello squirrel. Shouldn't you be busy collecting nuts for the winter?'
The squirrel said:

> 'That isn't fun
> I'm going to play
> I'll gather my acorns
> another day.'

So all that day the squirrel and the frog played games. They jumped over the stream till they were both tired. In the evening the squirrel ran home through the wood. It was almost dark and the five little squirrels were already fast asleep after another busy day. The lazy squirrel curled up and dreamed about his happy day with the frog.

The next day five little squirrels said:

> 'Come with us.
> There is so much to do
> gathering nuts
> for the whole winter through.'

But the lazy squirrel said:

> 'That isn't fun
> I'm going to play
> I'll gather my acorns
> another day.'

He ran through the wood to a field. A donkey lived there, and when he saw the squirrel he said:
'Hello squirrel. Shouldn't you be busy collecting nuts for the winter?'
The lazy squirrel said:

> 'That isn't fun
> I'm going to play
> I'll gather my acorns
> another day.'

That day the donkey and the squirrel had a wonderful time. The squirrel sat on the donkey's back, and they galloped round and round the field. At last they were tired. It was dark when the squirrel ran home. He crept up the tree and snuggled into his warm bed.

All through the autumn the leaves, acorns and nuts fell to the ground. Soon the trees were bare. All through the autumn five little squirrels were busy gathering acorns and nuts and hiding them in secret places. They were happy because they had plenty of food for the cold winter months.

One cold morning six little squirrels ran down the trees to the ground. It was cold and hard. The leaves lay in brown piles under the trees. They said: 'Brr! It's too cold to be outside today.'

So five little squirrels took some nuts from their winter stores and curled up in their cosy beds.

The lazy squirrel shivered. He was cold and hungry. He scurried around looking for something to eat. He looked on the ground and on the branches, but there were no acorns or nuts left. He sat sadly, wondering how he would manage all through the winter without a special store of food.

'What a silly squirrel I am,' he said. 'I should have been busy gathering acorns and nuts.'

He sat down and started to cry.

Suddenly five little squirrels scampered down from the tree tops. They said: 'Come along little squirrel. We have gathered plenty of food. There is enough for you too.'

They showed the lazy squirrel their hiding places, full of good things to eat. The lazy squirrel was so happy.

'How kind you are to share with me,' he said.

All through the cold winter six little squirrels had plenty to eat. The following autumn the lazy squirrel remembered what a silly squirrel he had been. He worked even harder than the five busy squirrels, and he was never lazy again.

Mr Smith's Black Hat

MR SMITH WENT for a walk in the park. He wore his best black hat. It was a sunny day, so Mr Smith bought an icecream and sat on a park bench. He took off his best black hat and put it next to him. He ate his icecream and closed his eyes. Soon his head nodded forward and he fell asleep in the sunshine.

A small dog passed by. He saw Mr Smith on the park bench, and he saw the black hat next to him.

'I'll have some fun with that hat,' said the dog to himself. He jumped up and snatched the hat away. Then he ran across the grass.

When Mr Smith woke up he looked everywhere for his best black hat. He looked on the bench and under the bench, he walked along the path and looked behind the trees, but of course he couldn't find it.

'Oh dear,' he said crossly. 'I have lost my favourite hat.'

He walked home sadly to tell his wife.

Meanwhile the little dog was having a wonderful game with the black hat. He tossed it and caught it and shook it till his teeth rattled. Then he remembered the juicy bone he had buried the day before. He dropped the hat and ran home.

The black hat lay on the grass. Suddenly four little boys passed by. They were on their way home from school. One of them saw the hat and shouted.

'Let's see who can kick that old hat the highest.'

The boys ran towards the hat, laughing and shouting. They took turns to kick it as high as they could. The poor black hat was muddy and battered. One of the boys kicked the hat so high it spun in the air and landed in the branches of a tree.

'Never mind,' the boy said. 'Let's go home. It's teatime.'

So the boys ran out of the park and left the poor black hat in the tree.

'Oh dear,' said the hat to himself. 'Whatever is going to happen now?'

Mr and Mrs Blackbird were flying in and out of the branches, looking for somewhere to build their nest. When he saw the black hat Mr Blackbird said, 'What a good place to build a cosy nest.'

The blackbirds flew to and fro collecting grass, leaves and twigs. They worked very hard and soon there was a comfortable nest tucked into Mr Smith's best black hat.

Over the next few days Mrs Blackbird laid four tiny blue speckled eggs. When the wind blew through the trees she was snug and warm in the nest in the black hat. She cuddled her eggs until four little chicks hatched out. The baby blackbirds chirped and chattered all day. Mr and Mrs Blackbird were very busy finding insects and worms for them. Whenever the babies saw a tasty snack four little mouths would open wide.

Soon the babies were so strong they were able to sit on the brim of the hat while Mr Blackbird taught them to fly.

'Don't fly too far at first,' Daddy Blackbird said.

So they flew to the next branch the first day. The next day they flew to a nearby hedge, and the day after that they flew around the park. The next day four little baby blackbirds left the nest for ever, and Mr and Mrs Blackbird said goodbye to the nest in the black hat and flew away.

Mr Smith's black hat sat sadly in the tree.

'I wonder what will happen to me now,' he said.

That night the wind blew. It blew so hard it shook the branches of the tree, and the black hat fell out. The nest fell down, down, down to the ground, and the black hat was blown this way and that, all through the dark night.

'Where are you taking me Mr Wind?' cried the hat.

In the morning the wind had stopped blowing and the black hat was sitting by a duckpond. Tiny rain drops fell into the hat, plip, plop, plip, plop, until it was full of sparkling water. Two frogs were sitting on a stone nearby. They hopped over to the hat and looked at it curiously.

'This is our very own pond,' they croaked.

They had a happy time sitting on the brim, leaping in and out of the water. It was a warm day, the sun shone and slowly the water in the hat dried up. At last there was only a trickle at the bottom.

'Come on,' croaked one of the frogs. 'Let's go back to the pond.' So they leaped away.

The hat was very sad. 'No one wants me for long,' he said. 'I wish I could find somewhere to stay forever.'

Just then a farmer drove by the duckpond on his tractor. He saw the black hat on the ground.

'That battered old hat is just what my scarecrow needs,' he said. He picked up the hat and threw it into the trailer. Then he jumped back into the tractor and drove into a large field. In the middle of the field stood a scarecrow. He was standing there to frighten the birds, to stop them eating the seeds the farmer had planted. He was very smart.

His head was made of a turnip and he had two wooden arms and one wooden leg. The farmer had painted a big red smile and two black eyes on the scarecrow's face. He wore an old jacket, a pair of gloves and a scarf, but he had no hat. The farmer took the black hat out of the trailer and put it on the scarecrow's head.

'There you are Mr Scarecrow,' he said. 'Now you are the smartest scarecrow on the farm.'

The black hat felt very happy to have found a new home. The scarecrow was very happy to be wearing such a smart hat, and he worked harder than ever frightening the birds away.

Mr Smith often wondered what had happened to his best black hat. He bought a new one, but he never again left it on a park bench while he fell asleep in the sun.

A Home In The Oak Tree

A BIG OLD oak tree stood in a wood. It was such a big tree that the strong wind which made the other trees sway hardly stirred its branches. All through the summer the oak tree was covered with shiny green leaves. In the autumn they changed colour and fluttered to the ground with hundreds of acorns. In the winter when its branches were bare the oak tree would dream about spring time when the warm sun would wake the hard brown buds and the leaves would grow again.

One spring morning a tiny brown mouse scuttled through the wood. He hurried here and there, to and fro, looking for somewhere to live. He ran round and round the oak tree and saw a little hole between the roots. He crept inside. It was dark and warm.

'This cosy hole is just right for me,' he squeaked. 'But a little mouse shouldn't live alone in a big oak tree. I'll go and find a friend to share my home.'

The tiny brown mouse hurried here and there, to and fro, until he saw a squirrel. The squirrel was running up and down a tree and jumping from branch to branch.

'Hello little mouse,' called the squirrel. 'I'm looking for a good place to build my house.'

Of course the mouse knew the perfect place. He said,

> 'Come little squirrel,
> come with me,
> build your home
> in the old oak tree.'

The squirrel followed the mouse as he scurried back to the old oak tree. The squirrel ran up the trunk and leaped from branch to branch.

He said, 'This is a wonderful place to build my home. You are a clever little mouse.'

The mouse said, 'A mouse and a squirrel shouldn't live alone in such a big tree. I'll go and find another friend to share our home.'

The brown mouse hurried here and there, to and fro, until he met a big black spider. The spider was sitting on a stone.

'Hello little mouse,' he said. 'I'm looking for a good place to spin my web.'

Of course the mouse knew the perfect place. He said,

> 'Come little spider,
> come with me,
> spin your web
> in the old oak tree.'

The spider followed the mouse as he scurried back to the old oak tree. The spider crawled from leaf to leaf and said, 'This is a wonderful place to spin a web. You are a clever little mouse.'

The mouse said, 'A mouse, a squirrel and a spider shouldn't live alone in such a big tree. I'll go and find another friend to share our home.'

The brown mouse hurried here and there, to and fro, until he met a prickly hedgehog sniffing among the leaves on the ground.

'Hello little mouse,' said the hedgehog. 'I'm looking for a pile of leaves to make a cosy home.'

Of course the little mouse knew the perfect place. He said,

> 'Come little hedgehog,
> come with me,
> there are piles of leaves
> by the old oak tree.'

The hedgehog followed the mouse as he scurried back to the old oak tree. The hedgehog sniffed at the piles of old leaves under the tree and said, 'This is a wonderful place for a hedgehog to sleep. You are a clever little mouse.'

The mouse said, 'A mouse, a squirrel, a spider and a hedgehog shouldn't live alone in such a big tree. I'll go and find another friend to share our home.'

The brown mouse hurried here and there, to and fro, until he saw a blackbird sitting in a hedge. The blackbird said, 'Hello little mouse. I'm looking for a place to build a nest.'

Of course the little mouse knew the perfect place. He said,

> 'Come little blackbird,
> come with me,
> build your nest
> in the old oak tree.'

The blackbird flew behind the mouse as he scurried back to the old oak tree. The blackbird flew in and out of the branches and said, 'This is a wonderful place to build a nest. You are a clever little mouse.'

The mouse said, 'Now I have plenty of friends to share my home. A mouse, a squirrel, a spider, a hedgehog and a blackbird can live together very happily in an old oak tree.'

Then he hurried into his cosy little hole and started to make it comfortable with bits of grass and moss. The squirrel gathered twigs together to build a snug home among the strong branches. The spider was busy spinning a web between the leaves and the hedgehog wriggled his prickles under a carpet of dead leaves. The blackbird sang a merry song as he flew about collecting bits and pieces to build his nest in the tree top.

Only the oak tree was still, sleeping in the sunshine and happy that so many friends were living together under his shady branches.

The Little Red Bicycle

MR SMITH WENT everywhere on his shiny red bicycle. It was rather old, but he cleaned it every week, and it looked as good as new. He polished it till its red paint shone and its chrome sparkled. It had a comfortable leather saddle, a large basket in front, and a shiny bell which Mr Smith rang merrily as he rode along.

One day, as Mr Smith was riding the red bicycle to town, he was overtaken by a big yellow bus. The bus was full of passengers going to the shops. As the yellow bus passed by he beeped his horn rudely and called,

'You are so slow little red bicycle. I'll be in town long before you.'

The red bicycle didn't care! Mr Smith kept peddling and the wheels kept turning.

A little further on he was overtaken again. This time it was by a fast blue sports car. Inside it was a smart young man going to work. The car slowed down as he passed the bicycle and beeped his horn noisily. The car called,

'You are so slow, little red bicycle. I'll be in town long before you.' He revved his engine proudly and sped on.

The red bicycle didn't care! Mr Smith kept peddling and the wheels kept turning.

A little further on the bicycle came to the bottom of a steep hill. Mr Smith had to peddle very hard, and the red bicycle struggled to the top of the hill. Suddenly a large car pulling a smart green caravan drove past.

'Silly little bicycle,' called the caravan as he sped by. 'Can't you manage the hill? I'll be in town long before you.'

The red bicycle didn't care! Mr Smith kept peddling and the wheels kept turning.

They reached the top of the hill at last and sped down the other side.

'This is fun,' said the little red bicycle. 'I love to go fast. Whee!!'

'You can't go as fast as me,' called an icecream van as it overtook him. 'You are so slow, red bicycle. I'll be in town long before you.'

The red bicycle didn't care! Mr Smith kept peddling and the wheels kept turning.

Soon they arrived in the town. The yellow bus, the blue sports car, the green caravan and the icecream van were already there.

'Old slow coach!' they called unkindly when they saw the red bicycle. 'You are always last.'

The red bicycle didn't care! Mr Smith did his shopping and filled up the bicycle basket. Then he rode home.

The next day the sun was shining in a clear blue sky. Mr Smith stood in his garden.

'What a lovely day,' he said. 'I think I'll go to the seaside.'

He packed his swimming trunks, towel and sandwiches into the bicycle basket. Then he set off.

It was such a hot day that a lot of other people had also decided to go to the seaside. The roads were very busy indeed. Soon the traffic was crawling along slowly and then it stopped altogether. There was an enormous traffic jam all the way to the seaside. Mr Smith and the little red bicycle didn't care! Mr Smith kept peddling and the wheels kept turning. They overtook the traffic, and Mr Smith rang his bell loudly.

Soon the red bicycle saw the big yellow bus ahead. It was full of passengers. Mums and Dads and boys and girls were going

to the seaside. They felt hot and cross, and the driver beeped his horn impatiently.
  The little red bicycle called, 'You are so slow yellow bus. I'll be at the seaside long before you.'
  The yellow bus looked down and was very angry when he saw the little red bicycle pass by.
  Mr Smith kept peddling and the wheels kept turning. Soon the red bicycle saw the blue sports car ahead. The young man looked hot and bothered. The red bicycle called,
  'You are so slow blue sports car. I'll be at the seaside long before you.'
  The sports car was very annoyed. 'Silly red bicycle,' he called.
  Mr Smith kept peddling and the wheels kept turning. Soon the bicycle saw the green caravan ahead.
  'You are so slow,' called the red bicycle. 'I'll be at the seaside long before you.'
  The caravan pretended not to hear, but he was very angry.
  Mr Smith kept peddling and the wheels kept turning. Soon they passed the icecream van. The driver was happily eating an icelolly, but the icecream van was so hot that steam had started to pour from under his bonnet. He felt even hotter when the red bicycle passed and called, 'You are so slow icecream van. I'll be at the seaside long before you.'
  Mr Smith kept peddling and the wheels kept turning. Soon they could see the sea, and in a little while they were at the seaside. Mr Smith parked his bicycle under a shady tree in the car park. Then he took his swimming trunks, towel and sandwiches and walked to the beach.
  The red bicycle settled down for a sleep in the sun. After a long time he woke up. The yellow bus, the blue sports car, the green caravan and the icecream van were driving into the car park. How late they were! The passengers climbed out of the bus. They felt sticky and tired.
  'Silly traffic jam,' they said. 'Next time we'll travel by train.'
  The smart young man jumped out of the blue sports car, slammed the door and walked angrily towards the beach. The people who owned the caravan were tired and the children were quarrelling. They set off to buy a cool drink.
  Something had broken down inside the icecream van, and

the icecream and icelollies were melting. The van felt very sorry for himself and the icecream man went to look for a garage to ask for help.

The yellow bus, the blue sports car, the green caravan and the icecream van all pretended not to see the red bicycle under the shady tree. They knew now that sometimes bicycles can arrive first.

The Yellow Umbrella

MRS GREEN HAD a brand new yellow umbrella. She was very proud of it and took it with her whenever she went out. Even on a sunny day she would open the front door and say,

'Well, it might rain. I think I'd better take my yellow umbrella.'

Then she would roll it up neatly and put it into her bag. Secretly Mrs Green always hoped it would rain. She loved to put up her umbrella and hold it high. She was quite sure everyone admired it very much.

One day, Mrs Green put on her coat and hat, picked up her bag and opened the front door. The wind was shaking the leaves from the trees, and tugging at the washing on the washing lines.

'What a windy day,' said Mrs Green. 'I'm quite sure it will rain.'

She put her yellow umbrella into her bag and set off for the bus stop. The wind tried very hard to blow off Mrs Green's hat. She put her hand to her head and held on to her hat tightly. When she arrived at the bus stop it started to rain.

'Oh good,' said Mrs Green. 'Now I can use my beautiful umbrella.'

She took it out of her bag, put it up carefully and held it over her head.

'Whee,' sang the wind playfully. 'Hello, yellow umbrella. Would you like to come for a ride?'

'Yes please,' said the umbrella. 'That would be fun.'

So the wind tugged and pulled at the umbrella. Mrs Green held on to her hat with one hand and the umbrella with the other. Then she took her hand away from her hat and held her umbrella with two hands. It was no use! The wind blew and blew. It blew her hat from her head and tugged her beautiful yellow umbrella out of her hands.

'Oh dear,' she cried sadly as she watched the umbrella sail over the roof tops. 'The wind has taken away my brand new yellow umbrella.'

Her hat was caught in a garden hedge. She picked it up and put it on her head. Then she climbed on to the bus.

'I'll never see my beautiful umbrella again,' she said sadly.

The yellow umbrella was having a wonderful time. He flew over the houses, over the chimneys and over the busy streets.

'I can see the shops,' laughed the umbrella. 'I go there every week with Mrs Green.'

'Whee,' said the wind. 'I'll drop you there for a while.'

The wind stopped blowing and the umbrella fell down, down, down and landed on the pavement. There were a lot of people rushing in and out of the shops with shopping bags. Feet scurried all around the yellow umbrella and he was afraid that he would be squashed. He rolled into the road. Cars, buses and lorries drove past and splashed him with muddy water.

'Oh Mr Wind,' the umbrella called. 'Please blow me away again.'

The wind came along. 'Whee,' he whistled and lifted the umbrella away from the busy street. He blew the umbrella high into the air.

'I can see the school,' said the umbrella. 'Mrs Green takes me there every day to collect her children.'

'I'll drop you there for a while,' said the wind.

He stopped blowing and the umbrella fell down, down, down and landed in the school playground. It was quiet and the umbrella rolled gently to and fro. Suddenly a loud bell rang and hundreds of children ran out of the school. They saw the umbrella and ran towards him to try to catch him.

The yellow umbrella thought he would be pulled to pieces.
'Oh Mr Wind,' he called. 'Please blow me away again.'

The wind came along. 'Whee,' he whistled and lifted the umbrella away from the laughing children. He blew the umbrella high into the air.

'I can see the park,' said the umbrella. 'Mrs Green and I go there to feed the ducks.'

'I'll drop you there for a while,' said the wind.

He stopped blowing and the umbrella fell down, down, down and landed in the duck pond. The ducks were very curious and excited when they saw the yellow umbrella bobbing up and down on the water. They pecked and quacked at him, until he was afraid that they would make a hole in him.

'Oh Mr Wind,' he called. 'Please blow me away again.'

The wind came along. 'Whee,' he whistled and lifted the umbrella away from the quacking ducks. He blew the umbrella high into the air.

'I can see the railway station,' said the umbrella. 'Mr Green goes there every day to catch his train.'

'I'll drop you there for a while,' said the wind.

He stopped blowing and the umbrella fell down, down, down to the railway platform. There were a few people waiting to catch a train. Some of them had large suitcases because they were going on holiday.

Suddenly there was a loud noise and the express train rattled into the station. It stopped slowly, shhh! The doors banged open and people jumped out. Other people climbed in. They were all in a hurry and rushed around the yellow umbrella without noticing him. Someone bumped him with a large suitcase and he was afraid that he would be flattened.

'Oh Mr Wind,' he called. 'Please blow me away again.'

The wind came along. 'Whee,' he whistled and lifted the umbrella away from the noisy train. He blew the umbrella high into the air.

'I can see the farm,' said the umbrella. 'Mrs Green takes me there to buy eggs.'

'I'll drop you there for a while,' said the wind.

He stopped blowing and the umbrella fell down, down, down and landed in a grassy field. The field was full of brown cows.

One of them came over to the yellow umbrella and sniffed him curiously. Then she licked him with her long pink tongue. The umbrella was afraid he would be chewed up.

'Oh Mr Wind,' he called. 'Please blow me away again. Please blow me home.'

The wind laughed. 'I think you'll be glad to be home after all your adventures. I'll blow you straight back,' he said.

The wind blew the yellow umbrella over the farm, over the railway station, over the park, over the school and over the town. He blew him over the rooftops and over the chimneys.

'I can see my house,' called the yellow umbrella.

'I'll drop you there,' said the wind.

He stopped blowing and the umbrella fell down, down, down. He landed in the garden and waited for Mrs Green to come home.

Mrs Green had finished shopping and was just opening the garden gate. She was very sad.

'I'll never have such a beautiful umbrella again,' she cried.

Suddenly she looked into her garden. There was her umbrella, her beautiful yellow umbrella. She picked it up. It was quite dirty, but almost as good as new. Mrs Green was very glad to have her umbrella back and the yellow umbrella was very glad to be home.

The Little Blue Tractor

EVERY DAY THE little blue tractor worked hard on the farm. He pulled the plough and the trailer and helped the farmer with all sorts of jobs. The farmer often said,

'I don't know how I would manage without my little blue tractor.'

Every week the little tractor had a rest while the farmer's son gave him a good wash and polish. When he had finished the tractor gleamed. Then he was driven into his shed, and he fell fast asleep.

One Monday morning the little blue tractor woke early as usual. He gave himself a shake and settled down to wait for the farmer.

'I wonder what jobs we will do today,' thought the tractor. He could see the sun shining through the window, and heard the birds singing in the hedge.

'I wish I didn't have to work,' he thought to himself. 'I'd like to have a day off. I'd like to have a holiday.'

He thought about this for a long time, and then he said, 'I'm not going to work any more. I shall run away.'

He waited a little while, and soon the farmer opened the shed door.

'Good morning little blue tractor,' he said. 'We have a lot of work to do today.'

He climbed into the cab and drove the tractor out of the shed. He jumped out of the tractor to close the shed door and the tractor said to himself, 'Off I go!'

He revved his engine and drove through the gate and down the lane. The farmer ran after the tractor shouting,

'Come back! Come back!'

But the tractor went faster and said,

'I'm a little blue tractor and I'm busy all day,
I'm tired of work so I'm running away.'

He enjoyed going along the lane in the sunshine, and he felt very happy. He came to a red traffic light and stopped next to a large bus full of passengers. The bus said,

'I haven't seen you before. Who are you?'

The tractor said,

'I'm a little blue tractor and I'm busy all day,
I'm tired of work so I'm running away.'

The bus was very cross. 'Everyone has to work,' he said. 'I work hard all day taking people to the towns and factories. I'm glad to be so busy. You should go straight back to the farm.'

The lights turned green and the bus drove away. The little blue tractor said, 'I don't care,' and drove along the road.

He stopped when a big red and white barrier came down. He knew this meant a train was coming and he sat still to wait. Suddenly there was a loud rattle and along came the train. When he saw the little blue tractor the train slowed down.

'Who are you and where are you going?' the train asked.

The tractor said,

'I'm a little blue tractor and I'm busy all day,
I'm tired of work so I'm running away.'

The train was very cross. 'Everyone has to work,' he said.

'I work hard all day taking people to the big cities. I'm glad to be so busy. You should go straight back to the farm.'

The train rushed away and the red and white barrier rose up high.

'I don't care,' said the little blue tractor and he drove along the road.

An orange and white police car with its blue light flashing overtook the tractor.

'Who are you and where are you going?' the police car called as he passed by.

The tractor said,

'I'm a little blue tractor and I'm busy all day,
I'm tired of work so I'm running away.'

The police car was very cross. 'Everyone has to work,' he said. 'I work hard all day chasing burglars and helping people. I'm glad to be so busy. You should go straight back to the farm.'

'I don't care,' said the little blue tractor and he drove along the road.

He passed a big fire station. The fire engines stood proudly in a row waiting to be called to put out a fire. One of them said, 'Who are you and where are you going?'

The tractor said,

'I'm a little blue tractor and I'm busy all day,
I'm tired of work so I'm running away.'

The fire engine was very cross. 'Everyone has to work,' he said. 'We work hard every day putting out fires and helping at accidents. We are glad to be so busy. You should go straight back to the farm.'

'I don't care,' said the little blue tractor and he drove along the road.

He passed a hospital. There were ambulances driving in and out with flashing lights and noisy sirens. Some ambulances stood still while sick people were carried out.

'Who are you and where are you going?' called one of the ambulances.

The tractor said,

> 'I'm a little blue tractor and I'm busy all day,
> I'm tired of work so I'm running away.'

The ambulance was very cross. He said, 'Everyone has to work. We work hard all day helping people who are ill. We are glad to be so busy. You should go straight back to the farm.'
'I don't care,' said the tractor and drove along the road.
Then he stopped suddenly. 'I do care,' he said sadly. 'Everyone is busy doing something useful except me. I'm going home!'
The little blue tractor revved his engine and drove quickly back the way he had come. He drove through the town and along the lanes. He drove through the farm gate and stopped in the farmyard. Then he beeped his horn noisily.
The farmer was in the farmhouse, feeling very glum. He was wondering how he would do all his jobs without his little blue tractor. Suddenly he heard the tractor's horn and ran to the front door. How happy he was to see the little blue tractor again.
'I'm so glad you've come home,' he said. 'I can't manage without you.'
The little blue tractor felt very proud. He never complained again and he enjoyed being so useful. He said,

> 'I'm a little blue tractor and I'm busy all day,
> I like to work, so here I'll stay.'

Mr Blue Tit Goes House Hunting

IT WAS SPRINGTIME. The sun shone in the blue sky and made everything look bright and cheerful. Little green buds poked up through the brown earth and tiny yellow leaves appeared on the trees.

Animals who had been sleepy all through the cold winter opened their eyes, yawned and stretched in the sunlight. Then they scampered away to find food. The birds woke very early and made a lot of noise as they started to build their nests. Soon it would be time for mother birds to lay their eggs, and they must build comfortable nests in safe places.

Mr and Mrs Blue Tit were looking for a special place to build their nest. They flew around the garden, peeping into every hole, hoping to find just the home they wanted.

'I think we should look for something different this year,' chirped Mr Blue Tit to his wife. 'I'm tired of draughty holes in trees.'

So he flew out of the garden, pausing on the way to nibble a tasty bit of bacon rind on the bird table.

'I'll come back when I have found just the right place for our nest,' he called to Mrs Blue Tit.

Mr Blue Tit flew over the hedge into the next garden. He saw a large wooden house with a pointed roof and a doorway at the front.

'That will do,' said Mr Blue Tit and hopped inside.

A large brown dog was asleep in the house. He opened one eye sleepily.

'What do you want little bird?' he growled.

Mr Blue Tit chirped

> 'I'm looking for a space,
> The very very best
> So that my wife and I
> Can build a little nest.'

The dog barked crossly and said, 'Go away. This kennel is my home. There is no room for your nest. You will have to find another place to live.'

He closed his eyes and went back to sleep. Mr Blue Tit hopped out of the kennel and flew onto the washing line. There was a garden shed nearby and Mr Blue Tit could see through the open door a large basket with a soft red cushion. It looked warm and cosy. He flew through the door and sat on the comfortable cushion.

'This will make a wonderful home,' he said.

Suddenly a large ginger cat and four kittens strolled into the shed. They had been for a walk around the garden.

'What are you doing in my basket little bird?' mewed the mother cat.

Mr Blue Tit chirped

> 'I'm looking for a space,
> The very very best
> So that my wife and I
> Can build a little nest.'

The cat hissed and said 'Go away. This basket is our home. There is no room here for your nest. You will have to find another place to live.'

Then she curled up on the red cushion and cuddled her four

tiny kittens.

Mr Blue Tit hopped out of the garden shed and flew across the garden. He perched on the branch of a tree and looked into a field. He saw a tall wooden house with a door split into two. The bottom half of the door was closed, but the top half was open and Mr Blue Tit flew inside. It was warm and smelled of straw.

'This will do,' said Mr Blue Tit and settled down on a large bale of straw.

Suddenly the bottom half of the door opened and a black horse trotted in.

'What are you doing in my stable little bird?' he neighed.

Mr Blue Tit chirped

> 'I'm looking for a space,
> The very very best
> So that my wife and I
> Can build a little nest.'

The black horse snorted and said 'Go away. This stable is my home. There is no room here for your nest. You will have to find another place to live.'

The horse put his head down and started to nibble the oats in a bucket.

Mr Blue Tit flew out of the stable and across the field. He saw a large stone building and flew inside. It was warm and quiet.

'This will do,' he said, and sat on a stool in the corner.

Suddenly a large herd of cows strolled in to be milked. They mooed noisily when they saw Mr Blue Tit and one of them said

'What are your doing in our barn little bird?'

Mr Blue Tit chirped

> 'I'm looking for a space,
> The very very best
> So that my wife and I
> Can build a little nest.'

The cow mooed and said 'Go away. This barn is our home. There is no room here for your nest. You will have to find another place to live.'

Mr Blue Tit flew out of the barn. He flew into the next field and saw a small house surrounded by a low wall. He hopped through the door. Inside was a fat pig with ten wriggly piglets.

'What are you doing in my sty little bird?' grunted the pig.

Mr Blue Tit chirped

> 'I'm looking for a space,
> The very very best
> So that my wife and I
> Can build a little nest.'

The pig grunted and said 'Go away. This pigsty is our home. There is no room here for your nest. You will have to find another place to live.'

Mr Blue Tit flew away sadly. His wings drooped and a tear dripped onto his beak. He flew over the pigsty, over the barn, over the stable, over the garden shed and over the kennel. He flew into the garden where he had left his wife, and sat on the bird table. He would have to tell her that he had not been able to find a special place to build a nest.

Suddenly he heard her singing and he looked up. She was flying towards a tree and her beak was full of grass. Mr Blue Tit flew after her and found her sitting in a hole in a tiny little house, high up in the tree top.

'Hello,' she chirped. 'A boy put this little house up after you had flown away. It is a perfect house for a family of Blue Tits.'

Mr Blue Tit hopped inside. It was indeed perfect. It was snug, warm and dry, and Mrs Blue Tit had already started to build a nest.

'What a clever wife I have,' chirped Mr Blue Tit proudly, and he sang,

> 'We live here
> and this is where we'll stay
> Our baby birds will live here
> until they fly away.'

The Lost Baby Blackbird

MR AND MRS Blackbird lived in a nest in a hedge. They had five baby birds. Every day they flew off to find food for the hungry babies. When they flew back with insects or worms five little beaks opened wide and five little babies cried,

'Me first, me first.'

Every time Mrs Blackbird flew into the nest she counted her babies. 'One, two, three, four, five,' she chirped, pointing to each one with her beak. 'Good, you are all here.'

One day Mrs Blackbird flew back with a big worm. When she had given the worm to the hungriest baby bird, she counted her babies before flying away again. 'One, two, three, four,' she said. She counted again, 'One, two, three, four,' she said again.

'One of my babies is missing,' she cried.

Mr Blackbird flew into the nest with a tasty caterpillar, which he gave to another hungry baby.

Then he counted them. 'One, two, three, four,' he said. He counted again, 'One, two, three, four,' he said again. 'One of the babies is missing.'

Mr and Mrs Blackbird were very sad. Mrs Blackbird sat in the nest and Mr Blackbird said he would fly away to look for the lost baby.

'Don't worry my dear,' he said to Mrs Blackbird. 'I'll bring our baby home safely.'

He flew over the hedge into a field. He saw a sheep eating grass, and a new lamb nearby. He flew to the sheep and chirped,

'My baby bird is lost. He is very small, but he can fly a little way. Have you seen him?'

'Baa,' said the sheep. 'I have been busy looking after my new lamb. I haven't seen your baby Mr Blackbird.'

Mr Blackbird flew to a high tree. There was a large hole in the tree and Owl was fast asleep inside.

Mr Blackbird chirped in a very loud voice. 'Excuse me, Owl. My baby bird is lost. He is very small, but he can fly a little way. Have you seen him?'

'Whoooo,' hooted Owl as he opened one tired eye. 'I have been asleep all morning Mr Blackbird. I haven't seen your baby. I'll look for him tonight when I am awake.' Then Owl closed his eye and fell asleep again.

Mr Blackbird flew into a garden. He saw a dog playing with a ball there and Mr Blackbird flew down to him.

He chirped, 'Excuse me, little dog. My baby bird is lost. He is very small, but he can fly a little way. Have you seen him?'

'Woof,' barked the dog. 'I have been playing with my ball all the morning. I haven't seen your baby but I hope you find him soon Mr Blackbird.' The little dog went back to his ball.

Mr Blackbird flew into a field and saw a donkey with his head in a bucket of carrots. He flew over and perched on the edge of the bucket.

Then he chirped, 'Excuse me, Donkey. My baby bird is lost. He is very small, but he can fly a little way. Have you seen him?'

'Ee aw,' brayed the donkey. 'I have been eating carrots all the morning. I haven't seen your baby.' He put his head back into the bucket and munched the carrots again.

Mr Blackbird flew into a farmyard. He saw a fat pink pig lying in the sun. He flew over to the pig and chirped,

'Excuse me, Pig. My baby bird is lost. He is very small, but he can fly a little way. Have you seen him?'

'Oink,' grunted the pink pig. 'I have been sleeping in the sun the whole morning. I haven't seen your baby.' He closed his eyes and started to snore loudly.

'Oh dear,' chirped Mr Blackbird. 'I must fly home and tell Mrs Blackbird that I can't find our baby. She will be so sad.' He flew back to the nest in the hedge.

When he arrived at the nest Mrs Blackbird was waiting for him. When she saw him flying alone she was very unhappy. Mr and Mrs Blackbird and their four babies sat in the nest wondering where the lost baby could be.

Suddenly two children walked along the lane. They couldn't see the nest because it was hidden in the leaves. One of the children said,

'Look, George. There is a baby bird on the ground under the hedge. Let's take it home to look after it.'

George looked and saw the poor baby blackbird lying among the leaves. It was very frightened and very hungry. 'No Polly,' said George. 'We must leave it there. The mother will find it and feed it where it is.' So Polly and George skipped away.

Mr and Mrs Blackbird heard what the children said and flew down from the nest. They were so happy to see their baby. He had fallen out of the nest when he had been trying to fly. After a little while he had fallen asleep and hadn't heard his parents calling him.

Mr Blackbird went to look for a fat worm for the baby. When he had eaten the worm and a juicy caterpillar the baby felt stronger, and Mr and Mrs Blackbird helped him to fly back to the nest.

The Blackbird family were very happy to be together again, and they all sang their best song to tell everyone the missing baby was home.

George and Polly had been hiding at the end of the lane. They saw everything that happened after they left the baby bird, and they ran home to tell Daddy and Mummy all about it.

The Noisy Donkey

SAM WAS A donkey and he lived on a farm with a lot of other animals. The animals were all good friends and Sam often left his paddock to visit everyone.

All the animals enjoyed Sam's visits because he was friendly and cheerful. Unfortunately he was also very noisy. 'Ee aw! Ee aw! Ee aw!' he would bray when he was happy or excited.

The little animals and birds were frightened and scuttled away to hide. The big animals said, 'Oh, Sam. Don't make such a noise!'

One sunny day Sam decided to walk right around the farm and visit all his friends. He trotted through the gate and went straight to the hen house. Mrs Hen was sitting inside keeping five brown eggs warm. She was waiting for them to hatch.

Sam put his head through the door and brayed, 'Hello Mrs Hen. How are you today? Ee aw! Ee aw!'

'I am very well,' clucked Mrs Hen, 'But please don't make so much noise. You made me jump and I almost cracked my eggs.'

'Sorry Mrs Hen,' whispered Sam and he trotted off to see Molly the brown cow. She was in the barn with her new calf.

'Hello Molly,' brayed Sam. 'I like your new calf. Ee aw! Ee aw!'

'Thank you Sam,' mooed Molly. 'But please don't make so much noise. My little calf is frightened when you shout so loudly.'

'Sorry Molly,' whispered Sam, and trotted off to the duckpond. Mrs Duck was swimming round the pond, followed by five little ducklings.

'Hello Mrs Duck,' called Sam. 'Your ducklings are so sweet. Ee aw! Ee aw!'

'Hello, Sam,' quacked Mrs Duck. 'It is lovely to see you, but please don't make so much noise. My ducklings are frightened and they have all gone to hide.'

'Sorry,' whispered Sam, and trotted off to see Henry the Horse.

Henry was old, and enjoyed grazing quietly in his field. 'Hello, Henry,' brayed Sam. 'Ee aw! Ee aw!'

'Hello Sam,' neighed Henry. 'Please don't shout. It's so peaceful here and all that noise gives me a headache.'

'Sorry Henry,' whispered Sam. He walked out of Henry's field, along the hedge and met Susie the sheep playing with her new twin lambs.

'Hello Susie,' brayed Sam. 'May I play with your lambs? Ee aw! Ee aw!'

'Hello Sam,' baaed Susie. 'You may play with them when they are bigger, but they won't want to play if you make too much noise.'

'Sorry, Susie,' whispered Sam.

He poked his head over the pigsty and saw Pansy Pig with her eight fine pink piglets. Before he had a chance to speak Pansy grunted, 'Don't make a noise Sam. My piglets are fast asleep.'

Sam crept away. He was very sad, and his long ears drooped.

'No-one wants to be my friend today,' he thought. 'Everyone says I'm too noisy, but I can't help it. All donkeys are noisy.'

He walked slowly to the farmhouse and saw Jip the sheep dog and Tibby the farm cat resting in the sun.

'Hello,' Jip barked. 'You look sad today Sam.'

'Yes I know,' answered Sam. 'None of my friends want to see me today. They all say that I am too noisy.'

'They are quite right,' mewed Tibby. 'You made so much noise when you met my new kittens they hid in the barn and it took me all morning to coax them out.'

Sam felt so sad that his ears drooped even lower. He walked

slowly back towards the paddock with tears plopping onto the grass.

As he passed the duckpond he heard a strange sound coming from the water. 'Miaow, Miaow.' He looked at the pond and saw one of Tibby's kittens.

She had climbed along an overhanging branch and had fallen straight into the water. Mother Duck and her five ducklings flapped around trying to help but the kitten was frightened and would soon drown in the deep water.

Sam knew he had to help and suddenly he had a good idea. He lifted his head, opened his mouth wide and brayed. 'Ee aw! Ee aw!'

It was so loud that the other animals heard him and were very angry. They all ran to the duckpond to tell him what a silly donkey he was. When they arrived at the pond they saw why Sam was making such a noise.

Jip jumped into the water, swam to the kitten and picked her up gently in his mouth. Then he swam to the bank and gave her to Tibby. 'Thank you Jip,' said Tibby, 'and thank you Sam. What a clever donkey you are, and what a good thing you have such a loud voice.'

Mrs Hen, Molly the cow, Mrs Duck, Henry the horse, Susie the sheep, Pansy pig and Jip the dog all agreed with Tibby. 'Well done Sam,' they said.

After that, no-one minded if Sam was noisy sometimes. They shook their heads when they heard the loud, 'Ee aw! Ee aw!' and said, 'Listen to Sam. What a happy donkey he is.'

And Sam never felt sad again.

Colin The Lonely Crane

COLIN WAS A tall red crane. He lived on a building site and he worked hard every day. The workmen were building a block of flats in the country and Colin was helping them.

Early in the morning one of the men climbed into Colin's cab and pressed a starter switch. Then Colin started to work. He picked up all sorts of heavy things and lifted them up to the workmen on the high scaffolding. Colin worked hard all day picking up blocks of wood and pipes and window frames. He was very busy, but he was also very lonely.

Colin was lonely because he had no friends. He was so tall that no-one bothered to talk to him. He looked down at the lanes and villages around the building site. He could see cars, buses and lorries rushing about greeting each other with friendly, 'Beep beeps'.

He heard the trains whistling to each other as they entered the railway station. The tractors on the farms chugged cheerfully to each other. Even the cement mixers on the building site chattered as they mixed the gooey cement.

Colin looked down at all the hustle and bustle far below and felt very sad. 'I am so lonely,' he said to himself, 'I wish I had a friend to talk to.' Big tears dripped down his metal frame and made puddles on the ground far below.

Colin was particularly lonely on Saturdays and Sundays because then the men didn't work. No one sat in Colin's cab, and there was nothing for him to pick up. The building site was quiet and the cement mixers were still.

One Saturday morning Colin woke up and felt sadder than usual. He had just decided to close his eyes and go to sleep again when he heard a voice close by his ear.

'Hello, who are you?' the voice asked. Colin was so surprised he didn't answer. He opened his eyes and saw a big blue thing flapping in the wind. It had a long colourful tail and was dancing on a long string which came from the ground. It had big eyes and a happy smile. 'Well, who are you?' it asked again.

'I am Colin the crane,' answered Colin. 'Who are you?'

'I am a kite,' the flappy thing answered, as it danced and fluttered in the wind. 'You look very surprised to see me.'

'I am surprised,' answered Colin. 'No-one has ever visited me before. I am too tall to have friends.'

The kite bobbed to and fro. 'I'll be your friend,' he said, 'but only on windy days. When it isn't windy I sit in the cupboard at home. When the wind blows I come out of the cupboard and have a wonderful time.' Colin looked down and saw, far below on a grassy hill, a little boy holding on to the kite's string. 'Will you really be my friend?' Colin asked.

'Yes,' said the kite, 'and I'll find you other friends too. Bye for now!' The kite fluttered away as the little boy on the hill started to walk home.

The kite was very kind. Whenever he went out to play on windy days he tried to find Colin new friends. Sometimes the little boy took him to the beach and the kite flew among the seagulls. 'Have you met Colin?' he would ask them. 'He is a tall friendly crane on the building site. He would be very pleased to see you.'

Sometimes the crane met little birds and he would tell them all about Colin as he fluttered in the breeze.

Soon Colin had lots of friends. All sorts of birds flew to see him. They sat on his frame and chattered and sang to him. Colin loved them all. Some of them even built little nests right at the top and he loved to watch the baby birds as they learned to fly. Sometimes the little boy brought the kite back to the grassy hill and he was very glad to see Colin so happy.

Colin was the happiest crane in the world and he was never lonely again.

The Five Ducklings

MRS DUCK SAT in her nest keeping five little eggs warm. She sat in the nest for a long time but one day she heard the special sound she had been waiting for. 'Crack!'

She waited and watched while five little ducklings broke out of the shells. Crack! Crack! Crack! Five little ducklings wriggled in the nest and looked around.

The ducklings grew stronger every day. One day Mrs Duck told them that it was time they learned to swim. They swam a little way the first day and then went back to the nest. The next day they were stronger so they swam a little further. Soon Mrs Duck was swimming round and round the duckpond with five little ducklings swimming along in a line behind her.

'Stay close behind me little ducklings,' she quacked, 'I don't want to lose any of you.'

One sunny morning Mrs Duck said, 'Today we will walk around the farm to meet the farm animals.' So Mrs Duck and her five little ducklings fluttered and flapped out of the duckpond and waddled along the path. 'Walk close behind me little ducklings,' quacked Mrs Duck, 'I don't want to lose any of you.'

'Quack, quack, quack,' answered five little ducklings as they waddled along behind her. Soon they came to a pigsty.

Mrs Pig was lying in the pigsty with ten fat pink piglets. She heard Mrs Duck call:

> 'Come and see my ducklings
> Quackety quackety quack
> We'll waddle round the farmyard
> Then we'll waddle back.'

So Mrs Pig pushed open the door of the pigsty. She admired the five little ducklings and Mrs Duck admired the ten fat pink piglets.

As Mrs Duck and her family waddled away Mrs Pig grunted, 'Goodbye little ducklings, please visit us again soon.'

One of the ducklings was very tired and couldn't waddle much further so he waddled into the pigsty, curled up between two piglets and fell fast asleep. Mrs Pig didn't notice the duckling in the pigsty and Mrs Duck didn't notice that one of her ducklings was missing.

Mrs Duck waddled along. She quacked, 'Walk close behind me little ducklings, I don't want to lose any of you.'

The four little ducklings waddled along behind her and said, 'Quack, quack, quack.'

They waddled to the meadow. Mrs Sheep was there with two brand new lambs. Mrs Duck called:

> 'Come and see my ducklings
> Quackety quackety quack
> We'll waddle round the farmyard
> Then we'll waddle back.'

Mrs Sheep admired the four beautiful ducklings and Mrs Duck admired the two woolly lambs.

As Mrs Duck and her family waddled away Mrs Sheep bleated, 'Goodbye little ducklings, please visit us again soon.'

One of the ducklings was very tired and he couldn't waddle much further, so he waddled back to the meadow, curled up between the two woolly lambs and fell fast asleep. Mrs Sheep was busy eating grass and didn't notice that one of the ducklings was still in the meadow. Mrs Duck didn't notice that now two of her ducklings were missing.

She quacked, 'Walk close behind me little ducklings, I don't want to lose any of you.'

The three little ducklings waddled along behind her and said, 'Quack, quack, quack.'

They waddled to the barn. Mrs Cat was in her basket with four wriggly kittens. Mrs Duck called:

> 'Come and see my ducklings
> Quackety quackety quack
> We'll waddle round the farmyard
> Then we'll waddle back.'

Mrs Cat jumped out of her basket. She admired the three little ducklings and Mrs Duck admired the four kittens.

As Mrs Duck and her family waddled away Mrs Cat mewed, 'Goodbye little ducklings, please visit us again soon.'

One of the ducklings was very tired and he couldn't waddle much further. He waddled into the barn, curled up in the basket with the kittens and fell fast asleep. Mrs Cat was washing her paws with her long pink tongue and didn't notice that one of the ducklings was asleep in the basket. Mrs Duck didn't notice that now three of her ducklings were missing.

She quacked, 'Walk close behind me little ducklings, I don't want to lose any of you.'

The two little ducklings waddled along behind her and said, 'Quack, quack, quack.'

They waddled past the field. Mrs Cow was there with two new calves. Mrs Duck called:

> 'Come and see my ducklings
> Quackety quackety quack
> We'll waddle round the farmyard
> Then we'll waddle back.'

Mrs Cow walked to the fence. She admired the two little ducklings and Mrs Duck admired the two new calves.

As Mrs Duck waddled away with her family Mrs Cow mooed,

'Goodbye little ducklings, please visit us again soon.'

One of the ducklings was very tired and he couldn't waddle much further. He waddled under the fence, curled up between the two calves and fell fast asleep. Mrs Cow was busy nibbling daisies and she didn't notice that one of the ducklings was asleep in the field.

Mrs Duck waddled on. She hadn't noticed that now four of her ducklings were missing and that there was only one left.

She quacked, 'Walk close behind me little ducklings, I don't want to lose any of you.'

The little duckling waddled along behind her and said, 'Quack, quack, quack.'

They waddled over to the stable. Mrs Horse was there with a new foal. Mrs Duck called:

> 'Come and see my ducklings
> Quackety quackety quack
> We'll waddle round the farmyard
> Then we'll waddle back.'

Mrs Horse trotted out of the stable. She admired the little duckling and Mrs Duck admired the foal. As Mrs Duck and the duckling waddled away Mrs Horse neighed, 'Goodbye little duckling, please visit us again soon.'

The little duckling was too tired to waddle any further. He waddled into the stable, curled up in the straw with the foal and fell fast asleep. Mrs Horse was busy munching an apple and she didn't notice that the duckling was in the stable.

Mrs Duck waddled on. She didn't notice that now all her ducklings were missing and she quacked, 'Walk close behind me little ducklings, I don't want to lose any of you.'

She waddled past the kennel and called to Bob the dog:

> 'Come and see my ducklings
> Quackety quackety quack
> We'll waddle round the farmyard
> Then we'll waddle back.'

Bob came out of his kennel. He had heard about the five new

ducklings and he was looking forward to seeing them. He could see Mrs Duck, but where were the ducklings?

'Woof, woof,' he barked, 'where are your ducklings, Mrs Duck?'

Mrs Duck looked around and saw that her ducklings were not close behind her. She started to flap her wings and quacked, 'I have lost all my beautiful ducklings.'

'Don't worry Mrs Duck,' barked Bob, 'I'll find them for you.' He raced away towards the pigsty.

'Woof woof,' he barked. 'Is there a duckling in there with you Mrs Pig?' Mrs Pig looked around and was very surprised to see a little duckling asleep in her sty. She woke him gently and took him out to Bob. 'Come along little duckling,' Bob barked, 'Mrs Duck is very worried about you.'

Bob ran to the meadow with the duckling waddling along behind him. 'Woof woof,' he barked. 'Is there a duckling in the meadow Mrs Sheep?'

Mrs Sheep looked around and was surprised to see a duckling asleep between her two woolly lambs. She woke him gently and took him to Bob.

'Come along little duckling,' he barked, 'Mrs Duck is very worried about you.'

Bob ran to the barn with the two ducklings waddling along behind him. 'Woof woof,' he barked. 'Is there a duckling in your basket Mrs Cat?'

Mrs Cat looked around and was very surprised to see a duckling asleep in her basket. She woke him gently and took him to Bob.

'Come along little duckling,' he barked. 'Mrs Duck is very worried about you.'

Bob ran to the field with the three ducklings waddling along behind him. 'Woof woof,' he barked. 'Is there a duckling in the field Mrs Cow?'

Mrs Cow looked around and was very surprised to see a duckling sleeping with her calves. She woke him gently and took him out to Bob.

'Come along little duckling,' he barked. 'Mrs Duck is very worried about you.'

Bob ran to the stable with the four little ducklings waddling along behind him. 'Woof woof,' he barked. 'Is there a duckling in the stable Mrs Horse?'

Mrs Horse looked around the stable and was very surprised to see a duckling asleep in the straw. She woke him gently and took him out to Bob.

'Come along little duckling,' he barked. 'Mrs Duck is very worried about you.'

Bob counted the ducklings. 'Good,' he barked. 'You are all here. Follow me.' He ran to the farmyard with five little ducklings waddling along behind him.

Mrs Duck was so pleased to see her ducklings again. She counted them carefully: 'One, two, three, four, five.'

'Thank you for finding my babies Bob,' she quacked.

As Mrs Duck waddled away with her family Bob barked, 'Goodbye little ducklings, please visit me again soon.'

Mrs Duck and her family waddled back to the pond. As they waddled along the little ducklings sang:

> 'We are little ducklings
> Quackety quackety quack
> We've waddled round the farmyard
> Now we'll waddle back.'

New Homes for Baby Rabbits

FOUR LITTLE RABBITS lived with their mother deep under the ground in a dark cosy burrow. There were a lot of other burrows on the grassy hill where they lived and every day all the rabbits played together.

The four little rabbits loved to chase and race each other through the long grass. When they were tired they nibbled the sweet grass and then slept in the sunshine.

Every evening all the rabbits who lived on the grassy hill ran to their burrows and crept down the dark tunnels to their underground homes. The four little rabbits curled up with their mother and slept till morning.

One day one of the little rabbits said, 'I'm tired of playing on this hill every day and I'm tired of sleeping in a dark burrow. I am going to find another place to live.'

'So are we,' said the other three rabbits. So the four little rabbits ran quickly through the long grass to the top of the hill and raced down the other side.

The first little rabbit ran as far as a leafy hedge and then stopped suddenly. He pricked up his long ears and listened carefully. He could hear something chirping among the leaves.

The rabbit peeped into the hedge and saw three baby blackbirds sitting in a nest. They all had their beaks open wide and Mother Blackbird was feeding them with insects.

When she saw the little rabbit Mother Blackbird chirped, 'Hello little rabbit, what are you doing here?'

The little rabbit said, 'I am so tired of playing with the other rabbits on the hill and sleeping in a dark burrow under the ground. Please may I live with you Mrs Blackbird?'

'Yes, of course you may,' chirped Mrs Blackbird kindly. 'I hope you will be comfortable in our nest in the hedge.'

All day long the little rabbit played with the baby birds as they learned to fly. They perched on a branch, flapped their wings and flew around the field. The little rabbit had a wonderful time running across the field and racing the baby birds back to the nest.

The second little rabbit ran as far as the stream. There were muddy banks at the sides of the stream, and smooth white stones made a bridge across the water. The little rabbit stopped running when he saw six green frogs leaping from the mud onto the stones and then into the stream.

When the frogs saw the little rabbit watching them, one of them croaked, 'Hello little rabbit, what are you doing here?'

The little rabbit said, 'I am so tired of playing with the other rabbits on the hill and sleeping in a dark burrow under the ground. Please may I live with you Mr Frog?'

'Yes, of course you may,' croaked the frog kindly. 'We hope you will be comfortable in our muddy home.'

All day long the little rabbit hopped from one white stone to another, right across the stream, and watched the frogs jumping into the water. Sometimes the little rabbit hopped onto the muddy banks and he washed his furry paws in the stream.

The third little rabbit ran as far as the wood. On the path between the trees he met a prickly hedgehog. The hedgehog was snuffling through the piles of dead leaves that lay under the trees.

When he saw the little rabbit the hedgehog said, 'Hello little rabbit, what are you doing here?'

The little rabbit said, 'I am so tired of playing with the other rabbits on the hill and sleeping in a dark burrow under the ground. Please may I live with you Mr Hedgehog?'

'Yes, of course you may,' grunted the hedgehog kindly. 'I hope you will be comfortable in my leafy home.'

All day long the rabbit hopped over the piles of dusty leaves while the hedgehog snuffled through them. The rabbit laughed when he saw the leaves stick to the hedgehog's prickly spines.

The fourth little rabbit ran as far as the farmyard. He stopped running when he saw a ginger cat with her five fluffy kittens. The kittens were playing with a red ball and tumbled over and over as they tried to take it away from each other.

When she saw the little rabbit Mrs Cat said, 'Hello little rabbit, what are you doing here?'

The little rabbit said, 'I am so tired of playing with the other rabbits on the hill and sleeping in a dark burrow under the ground. Please may I live with you Mrs Cat?'

'Yes, of course you may,' miaowed the cat kindly. 'I hope you will be comfortable in our basket in the kitchen.'

All that day the little rabbit played in the farmyard with the kittens and their red ball.

In a little while it started to get dark. All the rabbits on the grassy hill crept down the dark tunnels to their burrows and fell fast asleep. Mother Rabbit felt very sad without her four little rabbits and hoped that they were safe.

The first little rabbit was very tired after his exciting day with the Blackbird family. He curled up in the nest with Mother Blackbird and the three baby blackbirds. 'This is fun,' he said as he closed his eyes.

The second little rabbit was tired after his exciting day by the stream. He curled up in the mud with the six green frogs. 'This is fun,' he said as he closed his eyes.

The third little rabbit was tired after his exciting day in the wood. He curled up with the hedgehog under a pile of dead leaves. 'This is fun,' he said as he closed his eyes.

The fourth little rabbit was tired after his exciting day in the farmyard. He curled up with Mother Cat and her kittens in the basket by the kitchen fire. 'This is fun,' he said as he closed his eyes.

During the night the moon shone and the stars twinkled in the dark sky. The wind whistled through the trees and the leaves in the hedge rustled. The blackbirds were asleep but the little rabbit was wide awake. He was cold and uncomfortable in the tiny nest and the leaves in the hedge were tickling him as they moved in the wind. He missed his mother and his three brothers and the snug burrow on the hill.

Quickly he made up his mind. 'I'm going home,' he said. So the little rabbit jumped out of the nest, ran across the field and up the hill.

Down at the stream the six green frogs were asleep but the little rabbit was wide awake. He wriggled in the sticky mud and he felt cold and wet. He missed his mother and his three brothers and the snug burrow on the hill.

Quickly he made up his mind. 'I'm going home,' he said. He jumped out of the mud, ran across the field and up the hill.

In the wood the hedgehog was asleep but the little rabbit was wide awake under the pile of dead leaves. He was cold and the leaves were sticking into him. He missed his mother and his three brothers and the snug burrow on the hill.

Quickly he made up his mind. 'I'm going home,' he said. He crept out of the leaves and ran along the path through the wood. Then he ran across the field and up the hill.

In the farmhouse kitchen the cats were asleep but the little rabbit was wide awake. He felt too warm in the cat basket and the flickering flames in the fireplace frightened him. He missed his mother and his three brothers and the snug burrow on the hill.

Quickly he made up his mind. 'I'm going home,' he said. He jumped out of the basket, through an open window and into the farmyard. Then he ran across the field and up the hill.

The four little rabbits arrived at the top of the grassy hill at the same time. They were surprised to meet each other there in the middle of the night. They ran through the grass and found their hole in the bank. Then one by one they crept along the dark tunnel to their burrow.

Mother Rabbit was very pleased to see the little rabbits. 'I have missed you all so much,' she said.

The little rabbits were very happy to be home and they never left the burrow on the grassy hill again.

Poppet The Puppy

POPPET WAS A small black and white puppy and she lived with her mother in a kennel in the farmyard. Poppet's mother was a sheepdog and she was busy all day helping the farmer to look after the sheep. When Poppet grew up she would also be a sheepdog. Meanwhile she played all day on the farm and made friends with all the other animals.

One morning Poppet ran into the garden to dig up her bone. The farmer's wife had given it to her a few days before, and Poppet had been very pleased with it. She had chewed the bone all the afternoon and then her mother had helped her dig a deep hole and they had buried it in the garden.

When Poppet was in the garden she looked for the place where she had buried the bone. She ran to the apple tree. 'This is where my bone is,' she barked and started to scratch at the earth with her sharp claws.

The bone wasn't in the first hole she dug, so she dug another hole and then another. Soon there were lots of holes under the apple tree and lots of mounds of earth, but Poppet hadn't found her bone.

She sat down and cried. 'Someone has stolen my bone,' she

barked sadly. 'I must go and look for it.'

Poppet ran round and round the farmyard, wondering where to look for her bone. Suddenly she had an idea. 'Perhaps Mrs Cat has given my bone to her kittens,' she thought. So she ran into the farmhouse kitchen where the Cat family lived. Mrs Cat and her three fluffy kittens were asleep in their basket.

Poppet saw the cat bowls in the corner of the kitchen and ran over to see if her bone was there. She sniffed the bowls carefully with her wet little nose. One was full of creamy milk and the other held a tasty piece of fish. Mrs Cat woke up when she heard Poppet sniffing and she was very angry. She jumped out of her cat basket and hissed at Poppet.

'You naughty puppy,' she miaowed. 'Are you eating my fish?'

Poppet's ears flopped and her tail drooped sadly.

'I'm looking for my bone,' she barked.
'I want it for my tea
It isn't in the garden
Wherever can it be?'

'Well it isn't in my bowl,' answered Mrs Cat. 'Go and look somewhere else.' She chased the puppy out of the kitchen and then went back to her kittens.

Poppet ran round and round the farmyard and then had another idea. 'I'll go and look in the pigsty,' she barked. 'Perhaps Mrs Pig has given my bone to her piglets.'

Poppet ran to the pigsty. Mrs Pig was asleep with her eight fat piglets. They were all snoring loudly as Poppet pushed open the door. She saw the trough in the corner and ran over to it quickly. Then she started to sniff through the pigs' mash with her wet little nose.

Mrs Pig woke up when she heard Poppet sniffing and she was very angry.

'You naughty puppy,' she squealed. 'Are you eating my food?'

Poppet's ears flopped and her tail drooped sadly.

'I'm looking for my bone,' she barked.
'I want it for my tea
It isn't in the garden
Wherever can it be?'

'Well it isn't in my trough,' grunted Mrs Pig. 'Pigs don't eat bones. Go and look somewhere else.' Mrs Pig chased the puppy out of the pigsty and then went back to her piglets.

Poppet ran round and round the farmyard and then she barked,

'I'll go and look in the barn. Perhaps Mrs Cow has given my bone to her calves.'

Poppet ran to the barn. Mrs Cow was fast asleep in the straw with twin calves snuggled up against her. Poppet pushed open the door. She saw a box of hay in the corner and ran over to it quickly. Then she started to sniff through the hay with her wet little nose.

Mrs Cow woke up when she heard Poppet sniffing and she was very angry.

'You naughty puppy,' she mooed. 'Are you eating my hay?'

Poppet's ears flopped and her tail drooped sadly.

'I'm looking for my bone,' she barked.
'I want it for my tea
It isn't in the garden
Wherever can it be?'

'Well it isn't in my hay,' Mrs Cow mooed. 'Cows don't eat bones. Go and look somewhere else.'

Mrs Cow chased the puppy out of the barn and then went back to her calves.

Poppet ran round and round the farmyard and then she barked,

'I'll go and look in the stable. Perhaps Mrs Horse has given my bone to her foal.'

Poppet ran to the stable. Mrs Horse and her foal were asleep. Mrs Horse was swishing her tail gently to and fro to keep the flies away. Poppet pushed open the door. She saw a bucket of oats in the corner and ran over to it quickly. Then she started to sniff through the oats with her wet little nose.

Mrs Horse woke up when she heard Poppet sniffing and she was very angry.

'You naughty puppy,' she neighed. 'Are you eating my oats?'

Poppet's ears flopped and her tail drooped sadly.

'I'm looking for my bone,' she barked.
'I want it for my tea
It isn't in the garden
Wherever can it be?'

'Well it isn't in my oats,' Mrs Horse neighed. 'Horses don't eat bones. Go and look somewhere else.'
Mrs Horse chased the puppy out of the stable and then went back to her foal.
Poppet ran round and round the farmyard, then she barked, 'I'll go and look in the duckpond. Perhaps Mrs Duck has given my bone to her ducklings.'
Poppet ran to the duckpond. Mrs Duck was swimming round and round with six little ducklings close behind her. Poppet sniffed at the water with her wet little nose.
Mrs Duck swam to the edge of the pond when she saw Poppet sniffing the water and she was very angry.
'You naughty puppy,' she quacked. 'Are you drinking my pond water?'
Poppet's ears flopped and her tail drooped sadly.

'I'm looking for my bone,' she barked.
'I want it for my tea
It isn't in the garden
Wherever can it be?'

'Well it isn't in my duckpond,' quacked Mrs Duck. 'Ducks don't eat bones. Go and look somewhere else.' She flapped her wings at the puppy and chased him away. Then she went back to her ducklings.
Poppet was very sad and very hungry.
'Where is my bone?' she cried. 'Perhaps the sheep have it.'
Poppet ran up the hill to the meadow where the sheep were grazing and started to sniff the grass. Her mother was lying in the grass watching the sheep carefully to make sure they didn't wander away. When she saw her puppy she ran over and barked,
'Hello Poppet, what are you looking for? Why aren't you playing in the farmyard?'
Poppet started to cry.

'I'm looking for my bone,' she barked.
'I want it for my tea
It isn't in the garden
Wherever can it be?'

'I remember where it is,' said Poppet's mother kindly. 'I will help you look under the pear tree when I finish work today. We are sure to find it if we both look.'

Poppet pricked her ears and wagged her tail. 'Now I remember where my bone is,' she barked. 'I was looking under the apple tree and it was under the pear tree all the time.'

She raced away, ran into the garden and over to the pear tree. She scratched at the earth and soon found her bone. She was very happy and chewed it for a long time. Then she carried it proudly around the farm and the other animals were very pleased that Poppet had found her bone at last.

The Ripe Red Apple

AN APPLE TREE stood all alone in a field. In the winter its branches were bare but in the spring tiny green leaves started to peep through little brown buds. Soon the apple tree was covered in bright green leaves and beautiful white blossom. When the wind blew the blossom floated like snow flakes onto the ground.

In the summer tiny apples appeared where the blossom had grown. One apple, which grew at the very top of the highest branch of the tree, was the biggest apple of all. It grew plump and ripened quickly under the hot summer sun and soon it was red and juicy and ready to eat. The apples on the lower branches were still small and green and hard.

One fine morning a fat pink pig strolled into the field. He saw the apple tree in the middle of the field and walked over to it. He sniffed through the long grass under the tree, hoping to find a ripe apple that had fallen from one of the branches. He was disappointed not to find one, so he looked up at the tree to see if a ripe red apple was ready to fall.

Most of the apples were still green and hard but at the very top of the highest branch of the tree was the biggest red apple the pig had ever seen.

'That apple looks delicious,' grunted the pig. He jumped up and down on his short fat legs but of course he couldn't jump high enough to reach the apple.

At the top of the tree the ripe red apple bobbed up and down and said:

> 'No no Mr Pig
> You won't eat me
> While you are standing on the ground
> And I am in the tree.'

The pig walked away sadly and hoped he would find something tasty to eat in his pigsty.

A little while later a horse galloped into the field. When he saw the apple tree in the middle of the field he trotted over to it. He loved to eat crunchy apples and he sniffed in the long grass hoping to find a ripe apple that had fallen from one of the branches. He was disappointed not to find one, so he looked carefully at the low branches to see if there was a ripe red apple near enough for him to take.

The apples he could reach were still green and hard, but at the very top of the highest branch of the tree was the biggest red apple the horse had ever seen.

'That apple looks delicious,' neighed the horse. He stood on his hind legs and stretched his neck but the ripe red apple was still out of reach.

At the top of the tree the apple bobbed up and down and said:

> 'No no Mr Horse
> You won't eat me
> While you are standing on the ground
> And I am in the tree.'

The horse trotted away sadly and hoped he would find something tasty to eat in his stable.

A few minutes later a brown cow walked into the field. When she saw the apple tree in the middle of the field she ran over to it. She sniffed through the long grass hoping to find a ripe apple that had fallen from one of the branches, but although she looked for a long time she couldn't find one. She was very disappointed and hoped she would find a ripe apple on a low branch, but the only apples she could reach were green and hard.

Then she noticed the biggest red apple she had ever seen right at the very top of the highest branch of the tree.

'That apple looks delicious,' she mooed. She stuck out her long pink tongue but of course it wasn't long enough to reach the ripe red apple.

At the top of the tree the apple bobbed up and down and said:

>'No no Mrs Cow
>You won't eat me
>While you are standing on the ground
>And I am in the tree.'

The cow walked away sadly and hoped she would find something tasty to eat in the barn.

In a little while a billy goat trotted into the field. When he saw the apple tree in the middle of the field he ran over to it. He sniffed through the long grass hoping to find a ripe apple that had fallen from one of the branches, but of course he couldn't find one. He looked up into the tree and saw that most of the apples were still green and hard.

Then he noticed the biggest red apple he had ever seen right at the very top of the highest branch of the tree.

'That apple looks delicious,' he bleated. 'I will knock it down.' So he charged at the tree and rammed it with his hard curly horns. The tree swayed and its branches shook, but the ripe red apple bobbed up and down as merrily as ever and said:

>'No no Mr Goat
>You won't eat me
>While you are standing on the ground
>And I am in the tree.'

The billy goat was very angry and he ran out of the field hoping to find something tasty to eat in the farmyard.

In the afternoon a little boy walked into the field. When he saw the apple tree in the middle of the field he ran over to it to see if the apples were ripe. Of course the only apple ripe and ready to eat grew right at the top of the highest branch of the tree.

'That apple looks delicious,' said the boy. He picked up a long stick and tried to knock the apple down but the stick was too short.

At the top of the tree the apple bobbed up and down and said:

> 'No no little boy
> You won't eat me
> While you are standing on the ground
> And I am in the tree.'

Suddenly the boy grabbed a low branch and swung himself up into the tree. He climbed quickly from branch to branch until he had climbed high enough to reach the ripe red apple. He picked it from the top of the highest branch and put it into his pocket. Then he climbed down again.

The boy walked away from the apple tree happily munching the apple. When he had finished he threw the core into the long grass.

'That was delicious,' he said as he ran home.

And that was the end of the ripe red apple that grew at the top of the highest branch of the apple tree.

The Enormous Puddle

IT WAS A rainy day and big grey clouds covered the sky. Down on the farm everyone stayed indoors. The farmer and his wife sat in their cosy kitchen and had a cup of tea while they waited for the rain to stop. All the farm animals sheltered in the farm buildings and kept dry and warm while they listened to the pitter patter of raindrops outside. Even the ducks on the pond huddled under a bush and watched the rain splashing all around them. The rain fell all through the morning.

In the middle of the farmyard the rain had made a little puddle. During the morning the puddle grew bigger and bigger.

'Splish, splash, splish, splash,' said the raindrops as they fell into the water. Soon the puddle was enormous.

In the afternoon the rain stopped and left everything on the farm shiny and wet. The farmer looked through the kitchen window and said,

'It has stopped raining. I must take the tractor to plough the field.' So he put on his coat and hat.

'I am going to the market,' said the farmer's wife. She put on her raincoat and picked up her shopping bag and umbrella. Then off they went.

Out in the farmyard everything was quiet and still. The enormous puddle shimmered and sparkled.

In a little while Pink Pig came into the farmyard. He had been in his pigsty all the morning sheltering from the rain. Now he was going for a walk.

When Pink Pig saw the enormous puddle he was delighted and snorted happily.

'What an enormous puddle,' he grunted. 'It's just the right size for a pig.'

He walked to the edge of the puddle and sniffed the water curiously. Then he waded into the middle and started to blow bubbles with his pink snout.

'Oink oink! It's fun to play in puddles,' he said.

Sheepdog was asleep in his kennel. He didn't know that the rain had stopped but he woke up when he heard Pink Pig snorting and splashing.

Sheepdog ran over to the puddle and barked loudly. Then he jumped in, splashing water with his waggy tail.

'Woof woof! It's fun to play in puddles,' he said.

Pink Pig was very cross when he saw Sheepdog playing in the puddle.

'Go away,' he grunted. 'There is only room for a pig in this puddle.'

'No I will not go away,' growled Sheepdog. 'There is plenty of room in the puddle for me too.' So Pink Pig and Sheepdog started to quarrel.

Brown Cow heard them quarrelling and peeped out from the barn. She saw the enormous puddle and walked over to it. She mooed loudly and paddled at the edge of the water.

'Moo moo! It's fun to play in puddles,' she said.

Sheepdog was very cross when he saw Brown Cow paddling in the puddle.

'Go away,' he barked. 'There is only room for a pig and a dog in this puddle.'

'No I will not go away,' mooed Brown Cow. 'There is plenty of room in the puddle for me too.' So Pink Pig and Sheepdog started to quarrel with Brown Cow.

Black Horse looked out over his stable door. He was munching hay, but when he saw the other animals splashing in the enormous puddle he pushed open the stable door and trotted over to join the fun.

'Neigh,' he said as he kicked water with his hooves. 'It's fun to play in puddles.'

Brown Cow was very cross when she saw Black Horse kicking the water.

'Go away,' she mooed. 'There is only room for a pig, a dog and a cow in this puddle.'

'No I will not go away,' neighed Black Horse. 'There is plenty of room in the puddle for me too.' So Pink Pig, Sheepdog and Brown Cow started to quarrel with Black Horse.

Woolly Sheep heard the animals quarrelling and walked out of the meadow into the farmyard. When she saw the enormous puddle she was very excited and skipped into the water.

'Baa baa! It's fun to play in puddles,' she said.

Black Horse was very cross when he saw Woolly Sheep skipping into the enormous puddle.

'Go away,' he neighed. 'There is only room for a pig, a dog, a cow and a horse in this puddle.'

'No I will not go away,' bleated Woolly Sheep. 'There is plenty of room in the puddle for me too.'

So Pink Pig, Sheepdog, Brown Cow and Black Horse started to quarrel with Woolly Sheep.

Quacky Duck was swimming on the duckpond when he heard the commotion from the farmyard, so he waddled over and saw the enormous puddle. He flapped his wings and jumped into the water.

'Quack quack! It's fun to play in puddles,' he said.

Woolly Sheep was very cross when she saw Quacky Duck swimming in the enormous puddle.

'Go away,' she bleated. 'There is only room for a pig, a dog, a cow, a horse and a sheep in this puddle.'

'No I will not go away,' quacked Quacky Duck. 'There is plenty of room in the puddle for me too.'

So Pink Pig, Sheep Dog, Brown Cow, Black Horse and Woolly Sheep all started to quarrel with Quacky Duck.

They all squabbled so loudly and for so long that they woke up the sun who had been sleeping behind a grey cloud. He saw at once why all the animals were quarrelling and he was very angry.

'There is plenty of room in that enormous puddle for everyone,' he said.

The sun decided to teach the animals a lesson and he started to shine brightly. Soon the grey clouds began to melt away and then they disappeared. The sun shone so brightly in the blue sky that it dried up the rain drops that had fallen all that morning.

Slowly the enormous puddle became a small puddle, then a tiny puddle and soon there was no puddle at all.

The animals hadn't noticed the puddle drying up, so they were still arguing.

A blackbird had been sitting on the farmhouse roof all the afternoon. Now he flew down into the farmyard and said,

'Why are you quarrelling?'

The animals all answered together,

'Because there is not enough room for everyone to play in this puddle.'

The blackbird laughed.

'You silly creatures,' he chirped. 'The puddle has gone.'

Pink Pig, Sheepdog, Brown Cow, Black Horse, Woolly Sheep and Quacky Duck stopped quarrelling and looked down. Sure enough the enormous puddle had disappeared.

They had been quarrelling over nothing. They all felt very silly and wished that they had enjoyed the puddle while it had been there.

Quacky Duck waddled back to his duckpond, Woolly Sheep skipped back to her meadow, Black Horse trotted back to his stable, Brown Cow walked back to her barn, Sheepdog ran back to his kennel and Pink Pig went back to his pigsty.

The sun still shone brightly in the blue sky. When the farmer came back from the field and the farmer's wife came home from the market the farmyard was quiet again.

They never knew about the enormous puddle or about the silly animals who had quarrelled all the afternoon instead of having fun.

A Mouse In The House

AN OLD WOMAN lived all alone in a little cottage. She was busy every day. She scrubbed and polished and dusted until everything in the cottage shone. The garden was as neat and tidy as the house, full of the prettiest flowers and the tastiest vegetables.

One day while the old woman was digging up carrots, a tiny mouse ran into the garden. He ran up the garden path and in through the kitchen door. Then he sat in the kitchen twitching his whiskers and washing his face with his tiny paws.

The old woman carried the bowl of carrots into the kitchen and put them onto the table. Then she started to peel them and put them into a saucepan.

As she was peeling the carrots she heard something scuttling along the floor. She looked down and saw the mouse under the table. He was twitching his whiskers and washing his face with his tiny paws.

The old woman screamed and threw the carrot she was peeling up into the air. Then she scrambled up onto the kitchen table and started to cry noisily.

The old woman stood on the table for a long time. The mouse

found the carrot and he nibbled it with his sharp white teeth. After a while there was a loud knock on the kitchen door. The milkman had come to deliver the milk. When he heard the old woman crying, he looked through the kitchen window and said,

'What is the matter old woman? Why are you standing on the table?'

The old woman put her head in her hands and cried,

> 'There's a mouse in my kitchen
> He's been here all day
> Come in Mr Milkman
> And chase him away.'

The milkman looked under the table and, sure enough, there was the little mouse. His whiskers were twitching as he nibbled the carrot with his sharp white teeth. As soon as the milkman saw the mouse he dropped the milk bottle with a clatter and ran down the path shouting,

> 'I'm sorry old woman
> I can't help today
> I'm really too busy
> To chase mice away.'

He jumped into his milk float and raced away.

The old woman still stood on the kitchen table and she cried and cried. The mouse sat under the table twitching his whiskers as he nibbled the carrot with his sharp white teeth.

In a little while there was another loud knock on the kitchen door. It was the postman, and he had come to deliver a large parcel. When he heard the old woman crying, he looked through the kitchen window and said,

'What is the matter old woman? Why are you standing on the table?'

The old woman put her head in her hands and cried,

> 'There's a mouse in my kitchen
> He's been here all day
> Come in Mr Postman
> And chase him away.'

The postman looked under the table and, sure enough, there was the little mouse. His whiskers were twitching as he nibbled the carrot with his sharp white teeth. As soon as the postman saw the mouse he dropped the big parcel and ran down the path shouting,

> 'I'm sorry old woman
> I can't help today
> I'm really too busy
> To chase mice away.'

He jumped into his post van and raced away.

The old woman still stood on the kitchen table and she cried and cried. The mouse sat under the table twitching his whiskers as he nibbled the carrot with his sharp white teeth.

In a little while there was another loud knock on the kitchen door. It was the baker, and he had come to deliver a crusty loaf of bread. When he heard the old woman crying, he looked through the kitchen window and said,

'What is the matter old woman? Why are you standing on the table?'

The old woman put her head in her hands and cried,

> 'There's a mouse in my kitchen
> He's been here all day
> Come in Mr Baker
> And chase him away.'

The baker looked under the table and, sure enough, there was the little mouse. His whiskers were twitching as he nibbled the carrot with his sharp white teeth.

As soon as the baker saw the mouse he dropped the bread and ran down the path shouting,

> 'I'm sorry old woman
> I can't help today
> I'm really too busy
> To chase mice away.'

He jumped into his bread van and raced away.

The old woman still stood on the kitchen table and she cried and cried. The mouse sat under the table twitching his whiskers as he nibbled the carrot with his sharp white teeth.

In a little while there was another loud knock on the kitchen door. It was the butcher, and he had come to deliver some sausages. When he heard the old woman crying, he looked through the kitchen window and said,

'What is the matter old woman? Why are you standing on the table?'

The old woman put her head in her hands and cried,

> 'There's a mouse in my kitchen
> He's been here all day
> Come in Mr Butcher
> And chase him away.'

The butcher looked under the table and, sure enough, there was the little mouse. His whiskers were twitching as he nibbled the carrot with his sharp white teeth.

As soon as the butcher saw the mouse he dropped the sausages and ran down the path shouting,

> 'I'm sorry old woman
> I can't help today
> I'm really too busy
> To chase mice away.'

He jumped into his butcher's van and raced away.

The old woman still stood on the kitchen table and she cried and cried. The mouse sat under the table twitching his whiskers as he nibbled the carrot with his sharp white teeth.

In a little while there was another loud knock on the kitchen door. It was the window cleaner, and he had come to clean the windows. When he heard the old woman crying, he looked through the kitchen window and said,

'What is the matter old woman? Why are you standing on the table?'

The old woman put her head in her hands and cried,

>'There's a mouse in my kitchen
>He's been here all day
>Come in window cleaner
>And chase him away.'

The window cleaner looked under the table and, sure enough, there was the little mouse. His whiskers were twitching as he nibbled the carrot with his sharp white teeth.

As soon as the window cleaner saw the mouse, he dropped his bucket and ran down the path shouting,

>'I'm sorry old woman
>I can't help today
>I'm really too busy
>To chase mice away.'

He jumped onto his bicycle and raced away.

The old woman still stood on the kitchen table and she cried and cried.

'I think I will be on this table forever,' she wailed. 'Won't anyone chase the mouse away?'

The mouse sat under the table twitching his whiskers as he nibbled the carrot with his sharp white teeth.

In a little while the old woman heard something scratching on the kitchen door. It was a stray kitten, who was hoping that the old woman would give him a bowl of milk. When the kitten heard the old woman crying, he pushed open the kitchen door and miaowed,

'What is the matter old woman? Why are you standing on the table?'

The old woman put her head in her hands and cried,

>'There's a mouse in my kitchen
>He's been here all day
>Come in little kitten
>And chase him away.'

The kitten looked under the table and, sure enough, there was the little mouse. His whiskers were twitching as he nibbled the carrot with his sharp white teeth.

Suddenly the kitten ran into the kitchen with an excited, 'Miaow'. He ran towards the mouse, who dropped the carrot and scuttled away. The kitten chased the mouse round and round the kitchen and through the door.

They both ran down the path and through the garden gate. The mouse ran under a hedge and across the field, far far away from the kitten's sharp claws.

The old woman jumped down from the table and called the kitten back into the kitchen. She stroked him gently.

'What a dear little kitten,' she said. 'Would you like a bowl of milk?' So she gave the kitten a big bowl of creamy milk and he lapped it up.

Then the old woman went outside. She picked up the bottle of milk, the parcel, the crusty loaf and the sausages. She took them back into the kitchen and put them on the table. She put the window cleaner's bucket under the kitchen sink and then made herself a cup of tea.

When the kitten had finished his milk, he jumped up onto the old woman's lap and purred softly.

'You can live with me now, you clever kitten,' the old woman said.

So the old woman and the kitten lived together in the little cottage. The old woman gave the kitten a bowl of milk and a plate of fish every day and the kitten chased all the mice away.

A Day At The Seaside

IT WAS A hot day and the sun shone brightly in the blue sky. Down at the railway station Little Train was ready for another busy day. His red carriages had been polished until they gleamed and his windows sparkled.

The engine driver was in his cab ready to press the starter button. Every day Little Train chuffed through the villages, stopping at all the stations to collect the passengers who wanted to visit the town.

Today Little Train rattled happily along the tracks. The sun warmed his carriages and made his paint glow. Soon he saw the first station ahead.

'Whee!' he sang as his brakes slowed him down.

Farmer Giles was standing on the platform waiting for the train. He was holding two wriggly lambs which he hoped to sell at the market in the town. He climbed into one of the shiny red carriages. Then the station master slammed the door and blew his whistle 'Peep peep!'

'Off we go!' chuffed Little Train as he picked up speed. He rattled along past fields and farms until he saw the next station.

'Whee!' he sang as his brakes slowed him down.

Mrs Evans was on the platform waiting for Little Train. She held a big blue shopping bag because she was going to the town to buy her groceries. She climbed aboard the train and the station master slammed the door and blew his whistle 'Peep peep!'

'Off we go!' chuffed Little Train as he picked up speed. The sun still shone and made his wheels feel hot. He rattled along past factories and flats until he saw the next station.

'Whee!' he sang as his brakes slowed him down.

Mr Brown was standing on the platform waiting for Little Train. He wore a smart suit and hat and carried a leather briefcase and a newspaper. He was going to his office in the town. He was already hot as he climbed into one of the shiny carriages. The station master slammed the door and blew his whistle 'Peep peep!'

'Off we go!' chuffed Little Train as he picked up speed. The sun made his red paint feel hot and sticky. He rattled along past schools and streets until he saw another station ahead.

'Whee!' he sang as his brakes slowed him down.

Mrs Jones was standing on the platform waiting for Little Train. She was going to the town to visit the dentist. She stepped into a carriage and the station master slammed the door and blew his whistle 'Peep peep!'

'Off we go!' chuffed Little Train as he picked up speed. He could feel the passengers opening his windows to let in cooler air. Little Train rattled along past a big hospital and then he saw another station ahead.

'Whee!' he sang as his brakes slowed him down.

Mrs Green was standing on the platform with her smart white poodle. They were going to a dog show and Mrs Green hoped that her poodle would win first prize. She felt hot and bothered as she picked up the little poodle and climbed into the train. The station master slammed the door and blew his whistle 'Peep peep!'

'Off we go!' chuffed Little Train as he picked up speed. He rattled along past shops and houses. Then he saw another station ahead.

'Whee!' he sang as his brakes slowed him down.

Sam and Ben were standing on the platform waiting for Little Train. They were on their way to school and they each carried a heavy school bag.

'It's too hot for school,' they complained as they climbed into a carriage. The station master slammed the door and blew his whistle 'Peep peep!'

'Off we go!' chuffed Little Train as he picked up speed. The sun still shone and he felt tired and dusty. He puffed slowly to the top of a steep hill.

'It's too hot to go to the town,' he panted as he chuffed slowly down the other side of the hill.

Suddenly he came to a junction in the track. One set of tracks would take him and his passengers to the town, the other set of tracks would take them to the seaside.

'The seaside would be wonderful on such a hot day,' Little Train said to himself. Quickly he made up his mind and chose the track that led to the seaside.

The engine driver was very surprised and tried to stop him but Little Train took no notice.

In the hot dusty carriages the passengers were very angry.

'This isn't the way to the market,' said Farmer Giles as he tried to hold the two wriggly lambs.

'This isn't the way to the shops,' said Mrs Evans.

'This isn't the way to my office in the town,' complained Mr Brown behind his newspaper.

'This isn't the way to the dentist,' said Mrs Jones

'This isn't the way to the dog show,' said Mrs Green as she cuddled her white poodle.

'This isn't the way to school,' shouted Sam and Ben.

Little Train rattled along and still took no notice.

Soon all the passengers were banging the windows and shaking their fists, but Little Train wouldn't stop. He rushed through all the stations without slowing down. Soon he felt a cool breeze. A little while later he saw the sea sparkling in the sunlight.

'Whee!' he sang as his brakes slowed him down. Then he stopped.

All the passengers climbed out of the carriages and they were surprised to be at the seaside.

Farmer Giles rolled up his trousers and paddled in the sea while the two lambs skipped along the sand.

'This is better than going to the market,' he said.

Mrs Evans used her big shopping bag to collect pretty shells. 'This is more fun that buying groceries,' she said.

Mr Brown sat against a rock, put his newspaper over his face and fell asleep. 'This is better than working in my hot office in the town,' he said.

Mrs Jones found a rock pool and looked for crabs. 'This is more fun than visiting the dentist,' she said.

Mrs Green threw a stick for her poodle to fetch. 'This is much better than a dog show,' she said.

Ben and Sam built a big sand castle. 'This is better than school,' they said.

Everyone enjoyed their day at the seaside.

Little Train dozed in the sun and the engine driver dozed in his cab. At the end of the afternoon Little Train woke up. He stretched and rattled his dusty carriages and everyone climbed aboard.

Little Train rattled back along the track. He stopped at the stations and one by one the passengers left the train.

'Thank you Little Train,' they called as they waved goodbye. 'Thank you for a lovely day at the seaside.'

Little Train was tired and dusty but very happy. He puffed into his railway station and sat quietly while he was washed and polished. Soon his red paint gleamed and his windows sparkled again.

Tomorrow he would take his passengers to the town, but tonight he would dream about his wonderful day at the seaside.

Billy The Barge

EVERY DAY BILLY the barge chugged up and down the river. He worked hard carrying huge cargoes of coal to the power station. When he had delivered the coal he chugged back along the river to collect another load.

There were all sorts of boats on the river and they were all Billy's friends. There were motor boats and rowing boats and yachts and canoes. Sometimes a big boat sailed by full of happy passengers enjoying an afternoon on the river. Sometimes a police launch raced along the river with its blue light flashing and its siren wailing.

When Billy the Barge chugged along the river the other boats tooted their horns and waved their flags. 'Hello Billy,' they called. 'You are the busiest boat on the river.'

One sunny morning Billy emptied his cargo of coal at the power station and then started to chug back along the river to collect another load. He saw a white yacht sailing down the river on its way to the sea. Its paint gleamed in the sunlight and its bright blue flag flapped gaily in the breeze.

Suddenly Billy felt tired of carrying coal to the power station. He had always worked so hard that he had never had time to visit the sea. He made up his mind that he would go at once.

'I won't carry any more coal to the power station today,' he said to himself. 'I will sail along the river to the sea.'

He chugged along happily. All the other boats on the river noticed that he had not collected his cargo of coal and they called, 'Where are you going Billy?'

Billy tooted his horn proudly and said,

> 'I'm tired of the river
> I want to see the sea
> If I could sail among the waves
> How happy I would be.'

All the boats said, 'Be careful Billy, the sea is not as friendly as the river.'

Billy the Barge took no notice. Soon he sailed under a railway bridge. An express train was running along the track and he noticed Billy's empty cargo holds.

'Hello Billy,' he called, 'Where are you going today?'

Billy tooted his horn proudly and said,

> 'I'm tired of the river
> I want to see the sea
> If I could sail among the waves
> How happy I would be.'

'Be careful Billy,' called the train as he rushed into a tunnel. 'The sea is not as friendly as the river.'

Billy the Barge took no notice. An aeroplane flew down and he called, 'Hello Billy, where are you going today? Have you forgotten to collect your cargo?'

Billy tooted his horn proudly and said,

> 'I'm tired of the river
> I want to see the sea
> If I could sail among the waves
> How happy I would be.'

'Be careful Billy,' called the aeroplane as he flew away. 'The sea is not as friendly as the river.'

Billy the Barge took no notice. The river flowed on through a busy town. A car on the road called, 'Where are you going Billy? Where is your cargo?'

Billy tooted his horn proudly and said,

> 'I'm tired of the river
> I want to see the sea
> If I could sail among the waves
> How happy I would be.'

'Be careful Billy,' called the car as he stopped at a red traffic light. 'The sea is not as friendly as the river.'

Billy the Barge took no notice. The river flowed past a farm. A big green tractor was busy ploughing in one of the fields. When he saw Billy he called, 'Where are you going Billy? Aren't you working today?'

Billy tooted his horn proudly and said,

> 'I'm tired of the river
> I want to see the sea
> If I could sail among the waves
> How happy I would be.'

'Be careful Billy,' called the tractor as he pulled the plough along the field. 'The sea is not as friendly as the river.'

Billy the Barge took no notice. The river flowed on and on and soon it became very wide. Billy knew he was at the mouth of the river and would soon sail into the sea. He chugged on quickly. He was very excited because he could see the sea ahead and the waves were sparkling in the sunshine.

Billy the Barge had reached the sea at last! He had a wonderful time sailing over the tops of the waves. He played happily all the afternoon.

'This is much better than the river,' he tooted. 'The sea is the best place to be.'

Suddenly Billy saw an enormous ocean liner sailing towards him. 'Hello,' tooted Billy.

The liner looked down at Billy and blew its siren rudely.

'Get out of my way you silly little barge,' it shouted.

Billy chugged away quickly. 'What an unfriendly ship,' he said sadly.

A few minutes later a large cargo vessel sailed towards Billy. Before Billy had time to say 'Hello' the cargo vessel shouted, 'Get out of my way little barge. I am far too busy to bother with you.'

Billy the Barge was very disappointed. He had hoped to make friends with the ships on the sea. He thought sadly of all the boats on the river who were always so kind to him.

Now he noticed that the sun was sinking into the sea and that big black clouds were scurrying across the sky. The wind started to blow and heavy rain drops fell noisily into Billy's empty cargo holds.

Soon Billy the Barge was being tossed to and fro between huge waves. It was dark and he was very frightened. The waves crashed onto his deck and he thought he would soon sink to the bottom of the sea.

He saw a bright light winking at him in the darkness. 'That light looks friendly,' he thought. 'Perhaps I can stay there until the storm is over.'

He chugged through the angry waves towards the light, which sat on top of the lighthouse. Billy had never seen a lighthouse and he was surprised when suddenly it called out, 'Stay away little barge, or you will be battered to pieces on my rocks.'

Billy turned around and chugged away from the lighthouse as quickly as he could. All through the night he was tossed about by the waves, but at last the storm was over. The sun peeped over the horizon, the wind stopped blowing and the sea was calm again.

'I've had enough of the sea,' Billy said to himself. 'The river is the place for me.'

Billy sailed back towards the river. Soon he had said goodbye to the sea forever and he was sailing home.

The tractor, the car, the aeroplane and the train were glad to see him as he sailed by. 'Welcome back to the river Billy,' they called.

Soon Billy was chugging past all his old friends.

The little boats waved their flags when they saw Billy sailing back along the river. The passenger boat tooted its horn and the police launch sounded its siren. 'Welcome home Billy,' they called. 'We missed you.'

Billy was very happy as he waited to have his cargo hold filled with coal again. When he chugged along the river towards the power station he tooted his horn and called,

> 'I've been to sail among the waves
> I've been to see the sea
> But now I'm home with all my friends
> The river's the place for me.'

Sidney The Snail

EARLY ONE MORNING Sidney the Snail slithered along the garden path. He was very slimy. Two long antennae quivered as he slithered and his pretty black and white shell wobbled from side to side.

Suddenly Sidney saw a blackbird sitting in the hedge. Sidney knew that the bird was looking for his breakfast and that birds love to eat snails. So Sidney started to cry. He made such a lot of noise that a mole peeped out of his hole and said, 'Who are you and why are you crying?'

Sidney sniffed and said,

> 'I'm Sidney the Snail
> And I slither and slide
> That bird wants to eat me
> And I have nowhere to hide.'

The mole said, 'If you stop crying you may hide in my hole.'

'Thank you,' said Sidney and slithered into the mole hole. It was very dark and muddy and Sidney felt very uncomfortable. When the bird flew away Sidney slithered out of the hole and said, 'I want to hide from the birds in a house of my own.'

Sidney slithered across the grass. His antennae quivered as he slithered and his pretty black and white shell wobbled from side to side. As he slithered along he felt a drop of rain on his head. 'Oh dear,' he said. 'It's raining and I have nowhere to shelter.'

So Sidney started to cry. He made such a lot of noise that a caterpillar peeped out from the middle of a lettuce and said, 'Who are you and why are you crying?'

Sidney sniffed and said,

> 'I'm Sidney the Snail
> And I slither and slide
> But when the rain falls
> I have nowhere to hide.'

The caterpillar said, 'If you stop crying you may shelter in my lettuce until the rain stops.'

'Thank you,' said Sidney and he slithered into the middle of the lettuce and sat with the friendly caterpillar.

'Pitter patter, pitter patter,' said the raindrops as they fell onto the garden. Some of the raindrops fell onto the lettuce and dripped onto Sidney. The caterpillar was busy chewing a lettuce leaf so Sidney slithered away and said, 'I want to shelter from the rain in a house of my own.'

Sidney slithered across the flower bed. His antennae quivered as he slithered and his pretty black and white shell wobbled from side to side.

Suddenly he heard the wind whistling across the garden and saw the leaves being blown from the trees. 'Oh dear,' he said, 'the wind will blow me away.' So Sidney started to cry.

He made such a lot of noise that a cat ran out of the house and miaowed, 'Who are you and why are you crying?'

Sidney sniffed and said,

> 'I'm Sidney the Snail
> And I slither and slide
> But when the wind blows
> I have nowhere to hide.'

The cat said, 'If you stop crying you may shelter in my basket.'

'Thank you,' said Sidney. He slithered into the house and into the cat basket. When the kittens saw him they thought he was a new toy and started to play with him and scratched him with their sharp claws.

Sidney slithered out of the basket and said, 'I want to shelter from the wind in a house of my own.'

Sidney slithered around the garden pond. His antennae quivered as he slithered and his pretty black and white shell wobbled from side to side.

In a little while the sun started to shine. Soon Sidney felt very hot. 'Oh dear,' he said. 'Too much sun makes me feel ill.' So Sidney started to cry.

He made such a lot of noise that a frog hopped out of the pond and croaked, 'Who are you and why are you crying?'

Sidney sniffed and said,

> 'I'm Sidney the Snail
> And I slither and slide
> But when the sun shines
> I have nowhere to hide.'

The frog croaked, 'If you stop crying you may cool down in my pond.'

'Thank you,' said Sidney and he slithered to the edge of the water. He dipped his antennae into the pond and shook cool drops all over his hot slimy body.

'That feels good,' he said and he dipped his antennae into the pond again. Suddenly he overbalanced and fell into the water with an enormous splash!

'Help!' shouted Sidney as he sank to the bottom of the pond. The frog jumped into the water and dragged poor Sidney out. Sidney slithered away and gasped, 'I want to shelter from the sun in a house of my own.'

Sidney slithered around the rhubarb. His antennae quivered as he slithered and his pretty black and white shell wobbled from side to side. Soon it started to get dark and he had nowhere to sleep. So Sidney started to cry. He made so much noise that another snail slithered towards him and said, 'Who are you and

why are you crying?'
Sidney said,

> 'I'm Sidney the Snail
> And I slither and slide
> But when the night comes
> I have nowhere to hide.'

The snail laughed and said, 'You are a silly snail Sidney; don't you know that you are carrying your house on your back?'

The snail curled up and disappeared into his shell. Sidney was very surprised. He turned his head and looked at his pretty black and white shell. Then he curled up his black slimy body, tucked in his antennae and slithered inside. He felt cosy and safe and very happy.

'Now I can hide from the birds and the rain and the wind and the sun and the night in my own house,' Sidney said.

Then he closed his eyes and fell asleep.

The Happy Snowman

IT WAS WINTER and a cold wind whistled across the town. During the evening snow started to fall from the grey sky. All night long soft white snowflakes drifted gently to the ground. When morning came the houses and gardens and roads were covered with a deep layer of crisp snow.

A little boy built a snowman in his garden. He gave the snowman two bright blue beads for eyes, a long carrot for a nose and a happy smile made with orange peel. Then he put an old black hat on the snowman's head and wrapped a green scarf around his neck. The snowman looked very smart and the little boy was very proud of him.

'I'm sure that you are the very best snowman in town,' he said. Then he ran into his house for dinner.

The snowman stood very still at the bottom of the garden. He watched the busy street with his bright blue eyes, smiled his orange peel smile and said,

> 'It's good to be a snowman
> And watch the snowflakes fall
> The winter time when cold winds blow
> Is the happiest time of all.'

In a little while an old woman walked past the garden. She had been to the supermarket and she carried her heavy shopping bag carefully along the slippery pavement. She wore her warmest winter clothes, but she still felt cold and she stamped her feet to warm her toes. When she saw the snowman's happy smile she said, 'Hello Mr Snowman. Why are you smiling on such a cold day?'

The snowman smiled his orange peel smile and said,

> 'It's good to be a snowman
> And watch the snowflakes fall
> The winter time when cold winds blow
> Is the happiest time of all.'

The old woman shivered and said, 'I don't like the cold winter. In the summer the sun shines and my garden is full of flowers.'

The old woman walked home slowly. The snowman stood very still at the bottom of the garden. He watched the busy street with his bright blue eyes and smiled his orange peel smile. He thought about summer time when the sun shines and the gardens are full of flowers.

In a little while the postman opened the gate and walked up the garden path. He carried a heavy bag full of letters and parcels and posted one of the letters through the letter box. He wore his warmest winter clothes but he still felt cold and he clapped his hands to warm his fingers. When he saw the snowman's happy smile he said, 'Hello Mr Snowman. Why are you smiling on such a cold day?'

The snowman smiled his orange peel smile and said,

> 'It's good to be a snowman
> And watch the snowflakes fall
> The winter time when cold winds blow
> Is the happiest time of all.'

The postman shivered and said, 'I don't liked the cold winter. In the summer the sun shines and the birds sing.'

The postman walked to the next house with his heavy postbag. The snowman stood very still at the bottom of the garden. He watched the busy street with his bright blue eyes and smiled his orange peel smile. He thought about the summer when the sun shines, the flowers grow and the birds sing.

In a little while a policeman walked by. He was helping to direct the traffic along the icy road. He wore his warmest winter uniform but he still felt cold and he wriggled his toes inside his heavy black boots. When he saw the snowman's happy smile he said, 'Hello Mr Snowman. Why are you smiling on such a cold day?'

The snowman smiled his orange peel smile and said,

> 'It's good to be a snowman
> And watch the snowflakes fall
> The winter time when cold winds blow
> Is the happiest time of all.'

The policeman shivered and said, 'I don't like the cold winter. I like to go to the seaside on hot summer days.'

He walked down the road to help a car stuck in a deep snowdrift. The snowman stood very still at the bottom of the garden. He watched the busy street with his bright blue eyes and smiled his orange peel smile. He thought about hot summer days, and about flowers and birds and happy days at the seaside.

In a little while a big red tractor pulling a trailer full of hay passed by. The farmer was taking the hay to the sheep on the hill. Although he wore his warmest winter clothes he still felt cold and he wriggled his fingers inside his thick woolly gloves. When the farmer saw the snowman's happy smile he stopped his tractor and said, 'Hello Mr Snowman. Why are you smiling on such a cold day?'

The snowman smiled his orange peel smile and said,

> 'It's good to be a snowman
> And watch the snowflakes fall
> The winter time when cold winds blow
> Is the happiest time of all.'

The farmer shivered and said, 'I don't like the winter. I like to see the lambs skipping in the fields on warm summer days.'

The farmer drove on. The snowman stood very still at the

bottom of the garden. He watched the busy street with his bright blue eyes and smiled his orange peel smile.

The snowman stood at the bottom of the garden all through the winter. While the cold winds blew and the snowflakes fell, he dreamed about the summer. He thought about the sunshine, the flowers and the birds. He thought about happy days at the seaside and about lambs skipping in the fields.

One morning he woke up early. Everything felt different. The snow had stopped falling and a warm breeze blew across the garden. Soon the sun started to melt the snow and the snowman could hear water dripping from the trees. He smiled his orange peel smile and said, 'Summer is here at last.'

The snowman didn't notice that he had started to melt too. All through the morning he dreamed about the sunny summer days to come.

In the afternoon all that was left of the poor snowman was a puddle of water on the grass. Near the puddle was a bright green scarf, an old black hat, two bright blue beads, a carrot and a happy orange peel smile.